"You're here to meet a man."

The words dropped like stones on the lake. Kalinda swung her head to look at Rand, saw the cool fire in his eyes, and felt abruptly trapped by the power in him.

"It's business," she finally said, struggling to break the intensity of his gaze. "Personal, private business."

"You're not looking for a fling with me, because you're here to have an affair with another man. Don't you think it might be just a tad dangerous to amuse yourself with me while you wait for Mr. Wonderful to arrive?"

"Rand, stop it! You know nothing about the matter!" How could he guess so close to the mark? she thought grimly. "All we have is a casual acquaintance!"

"If these past hours are how you treat your fleeting friendships, I'd like to see what happens after you've known a man a couple of weeks!"

STEPHANIE JAMES

is a pseudonym for bestselling, award-winning author **Jayne Ann Krentz.** Under various pseudonyms—including Jayne Castle and Amanda Quick—Ms. Krentz has over 22 million copies of her books in print. Her fans admire her versatility as she switches between historical, contemporary and futuristic romances. She attributes a "lifelong addiction to romantic daydreaming" as the chief influence on her writing. With her husband, Frank, she currently resides in the Pacific Northwest.

JAYNE ANN KRENTZ
WRITING AS

Stephanie James

CORPORATE
AFFAIR

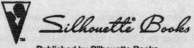

Published by Silhouette Books
America's Publisher of Contemporary Romance

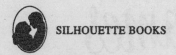

SILHOUETTE BOOKS

ISBN 0-373-80665-5

CORPORATE AFFAIR

This edition published by arrangement with Harlequin Books S.A.

® and TM are trademarks of Harlequin Books S.A., used under license. Trademarks indicated with ® are registered in the United States Patent and Trademark Office, the Canadian Trade Marks Office and in other countries.

Printed in U.S.A.

Available Titles From
STEPHANIE JAMES

A PASSIONATE BUSINESS
DANGEROUS MAGIC
CORPORATE AFFAIR
STORMY CHALLENGE
VELVET TOUCH
LOVER IN PURSUIT
RENAISSANCE MAN
RECKLESS PASSION
PRICE OF SURRENDER
AFFAIR OF HONOR
GAMEMASTER
RAVEN'S PREY
SERPENT IN PARADISE
BATTLE PRIZE
BODY GUARD
GAMBLER'S WOMAN

And coming soon...

TO TAME THE HUNTER
THE SILVER SNARE
FABULOUS BEAST
NIGHT OF THE MAGICIAN
NIGHTWALKER
THE DEVIL TO PAY
WIZARD
GOLDEN GODDESS
CAUTIOUS LOVER
GREEN FIRE
SECOND WIFE
THE CHALLONER BRIDE

One

It was the sound of his voice that first caught at her attention, tugged at her awareness. A deep, darkly timbered voice that elicited a curious desire to follow it and discover the man to whom it belonged.

Kalinda Brady walked hesitantly through the small, empty shop, her gray-eyed glance roving absently over the eclectic collection of watercolors of local scenes from the Colorado Rockies, wood carvings, and some woven wall hangings. The name of the little store was The Mountain Gallery and Kalinda had made three trips to it this morning before finding it open.

It was almost noon now and, not having much

else to do in the tiny, Colorado mountain resort
town, Kalinda had made one last trip down the
short street of rustic boutiques and crafts stores.
Sure enough, this time the owner had seen fit to
finally open his doors to potential customers.

But while the door stood invitingly open, there
was no one inside. A voice called to her, though,
as Kalinda tripped the shop bell.

"I'm out in the back! Yell if there's anything you
want!"

The masculine voice came through the door on
the far side of the small room and Kalinda walked
toward it, her curiosity getting the better of her.

She moved across the sunlit floor with an easy,
confident stride that said a great deal about her per-
sonality. At twenty-nine and with the recent success
she'd had of taking over the reins of her father's
firm in Denver, Kalinda didn't normally lack confidence. One couldn't and still retain leadership of
a major business. Still, her natural self-honesty
forced her to admit that thoughts of what she was
going to do this weekend here in the picturesque,
lakeside village sapped even her healthy store of
assurance.

But her outward demeanor remained unruffled
and coolly controlled. The chic, casual cotton tuxedo shirt she wore was open at the neck to reveal
a thin strand of gold around her throat. The shirt
was paired with khaki trousers done with a de-

signer's touch. The sophisticated tailoring revealed a slender, supple body. The high breasts were small but firm and gently rounded. The feminine hips flared with a fullness Kalinda had always wished was a little less so but which fairly screamed her femininity from within the confines of the narrow-legged trousers. The short, wooden-heeled sandals which arched her well-shaped feet came from Italy.

As she walked the sunlight filtering through the trees and into the window danced briefly on the wealth of brown-blond hair which had been neatly twisted into a knot behind one ear. The strict style revealed a strong, composed face, the features of which were less than beautiful. Instead of flagrant beauty, the intelligent gray eyes, straight, proud nose and readily curving mouth combined into a subtly attractive countenance which drew the attention of the more perceptive.

Kalinda wore both the expensive clothes and the inner assurance with a naturalness that spelled success. She had worked hard for that success and it annoyed her for some reason when others didn't work hard as well. Others such as the owner of The Mountain Gallery who didn't bother to keep regular hours. There was a look of mild disapproval in her eyes as she came to a halt on the threshold of the back door and took in the sight before her.

"I'll be with you in a minute. See anything you like?"

The owner of the heavily shaded voice glanced up from the body of a rainbow trout lying on a wooden bench. There was a stack of such unfortunate fish at the far end of the bench. A hose trickled water over the silvery scales as each awaited its turn under the knife. Kalinda unconsciously curled her lip in disgust.

"You're supposed to compliment me on the nice catch," the shop's owner informed her politely, hazel eyes laughing at her expression. "Not look at me as if I were an ax murderer!"

In spite of herself, Kalinda grinned in response. "Those poor fish are, I presume, the reason you're three hours late opening the shop?"

"If I'd known I had such an eager customer waiting I would have hurried," he drawled, the knife in his hand going to work efficiently on the fish in front of him. Kalinda looked away.

Her curious gaze rested on the bent head of the man in front of her, noting the dark fire in the thick, chestnut hair which was carelessly combed and a little long for her taste. The man stood naked from the waist up in the bright sunlight, his lean, smoothly muscled body well-bronzed. When she found her glance lingering on the curling red-brown hair which covered his chest and tapered down to disappear beneath the waistband of a faded pair of snug-fitting jeans, she looked away from that sight, also.

Which brought her gaze back to his profile. She found herself studying it with the same curiosity that had made her want to follow the sound of his voice.

It was an angular face, sharply etched and tanned like the rest of him. The hazel eyes were deep-set and flickered with intelligence when he glanced up and caught her watching him. Tiny lines crinkled the corners beneath heavy brows. An arrogant nose paired well with high cheekbones and a mouth which seemed hard in repose.

But the mouth smiled easily, she saw, and the deep lines at the edges bespoke a wealth of experience. She found herself wondering just what sort of experience, however. There was nothing polished or sophisticated about this man. And he definitely wasn't the sort she had expected to encounter running an art gallery, even if that gallery was in an isolated mountain town which catered to tourists. Her curiosity grew.

He must have been around thirty-seven or thirty-eight, she reflected absently. She sensed a latent male power in him and wondered how he could have been content to waste his life running a part-time gallery and fishing when the urge took him. In her world, given a little business experience, such a man could have built an empire. She knew it instinctively.

Well, hers was not to judge, Kalinda told herself

firmly, knowing she was doing it anyway. He was probably a leftover from the antimaterialistic, anti-establishment era of a few years back. A man who lacked the basic drive and competitive inclination it took to make it to the top.

"I wanted to ask about that watercolor of the lake hanging in the window," she told him politely.

"You like it?" he inquired interestedly, pausing in his work to eye her.

"I know someone who will," she temporized.

"You *don't* like it," he stated, nodding. He went back to cleaning the trout.

"I'm not buying it for myself."

"What's this friend like? The one you're buying it for?"

"Does it matter?" she asked dryly. "Are you worried the painting won't be going to a good home?"

"I'm not worried about it, but Mary Beth will be," he explained with seeming patience.

"Mary Beth being the artist, I presume?" Kalinda hazarded.

"Umm. She's very particular about who gets her paintings."

"I see. I didn't think artists could afford that sort of luxury. Tell Mary Beth that I'm buying it to give to a kindly, distinguished, older couple who grew up in Colorado and treasure scenes such as that one."

"I guess that sounds safe enough. Okay, you can have it."

"I can't tell you how thrilled I am that you're willing to part with it," she muttered, thinking if she hadn't been stuck in town anyway, she would never have made three trips to the gallery in order to buy the painting.

He laughed, a rich, full-bodied laughter that filled the yard in which he was standing. "Give me a chance to wash the evidence off my hands and I'll come inside and take your money. My name's Rand Alastair, by the way. What's yours?"

Kalinda blinked, surprised at the straightforward question from a stranger she never intended to see again. "Kalinda. Kalinda Brady."

He nodded. "On vacation?" He turned away to wash his hands under the hose, his body moving with a litheness Kalinda found unexpectedly pleasing.

"Not exactly," she replied unthinkingly and then wished she'd held her tongue. The last thing she wanted was a drawn-out discussion of her reasons for being in town!

"Business?" Rand pursued, coming toward her with a rather persistent expression.

"It's a personal matter," she replied, letting her annoyance show.

It didn't seem to phase him. "I see. Are you here by yourself?"

"I don't think that's any of your business," she told him gently, knowing any one of her employees would have immediately backed off after hearing that tone of voice.

To her surprise, Rand had the grace to wince. "Sorry, I still do that once in a while."

"Still do what?" Kalinda looked at him blankly, not understanding the remark. He led her back into the gallery.

"Never mind. Want a cold beer? It's going to get warm this afternoon."

She started to decline but Rand was already opening a small refrigerator against the back wall and rummaging around inside. He straightened with two chilled cans in his hand and popped the tops on both before Kalinda could think of a polite excuse. "Here you go."

She peered down at the can skeptically as it was thrust into her hand, then tried an experimental sip. It wasn't chilled, dry Chenin Blanc, but it wasn't bad on a warm afternoon in the mountains. She took another sip and glanced up to find her host grinning at her.

"Think of it as getting back to basics," he murmured and took a long, satisfying swallow. "Now let's see, I've got that price list around here somewhere...."

Beer in hand, Rand rummaged around in the drawer behind the counter, eventually producing a scrap of paper with a triumphant air. "I knew it was here!"

"Congratulations," Kalinda couldn't resist saying a little tartly. What a way to run a business! Any business!

He ignored the comment as if accustomed to the rudeness of visitors and gave her the price of the painting.

It was a bit higher than Kalinda had expected and automatically she glanced around to take another look at the watercolor landscape. As she did a charming pottery bowl caught her eye.

"Oh, I like that!" she exclaimed with genuine enthusiasm, walking across the room to lift the well-molded object. It fit nicely in her hand and the earthen colors were perfect for her dining room. "I can see this now filled with a lovely curry and rice dish or maybe a huge green salad."

She raised her head and found Rand watching her intently. "I'll take this, too," she said easily, carrying it back to the counter. "And you needn't worry about it. It's going to a good home."

"Yours?" he smiled.

"Mine," she confirmed, digging out her checkbook.

She hid a small frown as Rand calmly accepted her check without bothering to check her identification and then told herself it was his business. If he chose to take such risks who was she to tell him different?

"I'll wrap those in paper for you before you leave," he announced cheerfully, coming around from behind the counter.

"As a matter of fact," Kalinda said pointedly, "I was just about to go. Perhaps you could put the paper around them now?"

"Finish your beer first. Unless someone's waiting for you?" he added innocently.

"Well, no, but..." Too late she realized she'd just answered his earlier question about whether or not she was in town alone. Half-irritated and half-amused over the small trap, she met his laughing eyes.

"Believe me," he soothed, "there's not much else to do in town once you've been through the shops. Unless, of course, you're into fishing...."

"Not particularly," she sighed.

"I thought not. Come on outside and sit under a tree while I finish cleaning the fish. You might as well relax while you finish the beer...."

"Mr. Alastair," Kalinda began firmly, still unable to decide if she should laugh or treat him to one of her more repressive tones. But she was finding his unabashed persistence almost entertaining. And heaven knew she needed a bit of entertainment to take her mind off her own plans!

"Be nice," he pleaded with a beguiling smile

that weakened her further. "Everyone likes to show off his catch. And I can tell by looking at you that you're bored and restless."

"Is it that obvious?" she groaned, following him back out into the yard.

"Let's just say you look a little out of your element," he said softly, waving her to a redwood chair under a tree. "But don't fret, I'm relatively harmless. I can produce any number of local references." He picked up a fish and threw her a quick leer.

Kalinda took a long sip of beer and silently lifted one faintly quelling eyebrow. Rand didn't appear to notice. Instead he chatted amiably, his knife moving expertly on the trout.

Afterward, Kalinda had to admit she wasn't quite sure how it had happened, but she wound up sitting under a tree with a can of beer and watching a man clean fish until nearly one o'clock in the afternoon. No one who knew her back in Denver would have believed it. But then no one back in Denver could possibly know how desperately she was trying to kill the rest of this day and the next.

The light, easy conversation proved a tonic for her, succeeding in taking her mind off her inner, churning thoughts and giving her a temporary respite from the case of nerves she was in danger of contracting.

"What do you do in Denver?" Rand demanded casually at one point after giving her a humorous description of the life he led running a gallery in a tourist town.

"I run a company called Brady Data Processing," she admitted mildly, her cool confidence implicit in her voice. It was, after all, something she did very well.

"I've heard of it," he astonished her by admitting calmly. "You're in charge?" There was a speculative gleam in the quick glance he tossed over at her.

"I was elected chief executive officer a couple of years ago after my father was killed in a plane crash. I sort of inherited the reins. The board of directors was used to having a Brady at the helm," she shrugged. "I'm surprised you've heard of the company."

"We're not totally isolated up here," he informed her dryly.

"Could have fooled me," Kalinda laughed.

He swung around. "You are bored, aren't you? What are you doing here in our little burg, Kalinda Brady?"

"I think you already asked me that," she retorted blandly, feeling as if he'd almost caught her off guard with the question.

"And you didn't answer. Don't you know you're making me curious?"

"It will liven up your rather placid lifestyle."

He laughed, clearly enjoying the day and her. Kalinda felt herself relax and put her problem temporarily aside. More time slipped past until, conscious of having missed lunch, she finally stood up reluctantly and tossed the beer can into a nearby container.

"Well, thanks for the beer, Rand. I think it's time I was on my way. If you'll wrap the painting and the pottery, I'll..."

"I'll have them ready this evening," he drawled smoothly as he finished with the fish.

"This evening!"

"When you help me eat the evidence of my murder spree."

"Rand, I don't think..."

"Fresh trout? Grilled corn? How can you resist? And you've already admitted you're bored," he coaxed, hazel eyes fastening on her with determination.

Kalinda mentally ran through all the reasons she couldn't have dinner with him and found it a very short list. Why shouldn't she accept? She had a long evening to get through by herself if she refused and that thought wasn't very appealing. Alone with her plans and worries...

He met her eyes and smiled. Kalinda drew in her breath, aware that he'd seen the hesitation in her. Once again it struck her that this man might have been a formidable figure in the business world if he'd chosen that path in life. He knew how to manipulate others. Or was it just that she was willing to be manipulated that afternoon?

"All right," she agreed gently. "Thank you."

"I'll pick you up at six. My home is down by the lake," he said.

It wasn't until she had left the shop to return to her motel that Kalinda wondered which of them was intent on fighting off a boring evening. Could it be that Rand Alastair was a little restless, too? But that didn't make any sense. He had obviously chosen to live in this out-of-the-way town of his own accord. And he clearly enjoyed his fishing. Well, it wasn't her problem. She had her own!

She chose the perfect little summer dress she had brought with her, a wrapped and ruffled silk crepe de chine print. It was bare, breezy and, combined with strappy little sandals, even flirty in a sophisticated way. She left her hair in the sleek twist behind her ear and added a gold wire of a bracelet to her bare arm. She wasn't going out of her way to dress for Rand Alastair. Kalinda liked clothes and she dressed to please herself.

She was prepared to find Rand in a clean pair of jeans and a shirt when she opened the door to him a little before six, but the subtle, pin-striped shirt and dark slacks looked expensive and well-tailored. The thick, chestnut hair was combed back in a broad wave and there was a clean, masculine scent of aftershave clinging tantalizingly around him. Still, it was the white Lotus behind him in the parking lot which took Kalinda aback.

"Yours?" she murmured unnecessarily as he guided her toward it with a casually possessive hand at the small of her back.

"It was either this or the motorcycle," he grinned engagingly, "and somehow I had a hunch you'd object to the bike." His eyes ran approvingly over the little flirty dress. "Although it might have been interesting..."

"The Lotus is fine," she told him dryly as he slipped her into the cockpit of the low-slung car. Her eyes narrowed slightly as she watched him walk around the hood. The gallery must be doing better than it looked, she decided. But that didn't make any sense....

"Why do I have this feeling that I'm turning out to be a source of amusement for you?" Rand asked sometime later as he pan-fried the fresh trout over the open flame of a barbecue pit. The corn he was grilling alongside gave off an enticing aroma.

"Don't you want me to enjoy myself?" she retorted, crossing her slender ankles as she reclined on the outdoor lounger. The shaded patio was situated to take full advantage of the tree-rimmed lake and privately Kalinda knew the glass-walled house with its elegant, rustic lines had been another surprise to her.

It went with the Lotus, however. The wood-and-glass structure was obviously designed just for the particular, wooded, hillside lot on which it had been placed. The walk through the entryway and living room out to the patio had revealed a plush, cream carpet, low, sleekly styled caramel and brown furniture and a scattering of beautiful, earth-toned pottery pieces. Rand had merely smiled when she'd commented on them.

"Don't get me wrong," he said in response to her flippant question. "I'm delighted to have you enjoy yourself. It's just that I'd prefer the amusement to be a shared experience!"

Kalinda gave him a slow, teasing smile as she sipped at the tartly delicious concoction of apricot brandy, lemon and orange juice he'd prepared for them. "Are you artistic types always so sensitive?"

"Are you vacationing business executives always so condescending to the local peasantry?"

There was an edge on the darkly timbered voice that made Kalinda wonder if her new acquaintance might not appreciate knowing he was merely a means of getting through a difficult evening.

"You seem to eat rather well for a peasant," she murmured, glancing pointedly at the sizzling trout. "Off the land, as it were."

He grinned, a slashing, faintly predatory expression which sent a trickle of unease through her. Kalinda deliberately banished the unwelcome sensation. Rand Alastair was no threat to her and certainly not her chief concern.

"The trout may be free, but how do you know I didn't spend my last cent on the wine in a desperate effort to impress you?"

"Did you?"

"Not quite," he admitted, casting a rueful look at the bottle of Chardonnay chilling nearby.

"I didn't think so. That little gallery you run in town appears to be bringing in enough to keep you from starving to death," Kalinda commented.

"You sound as if you don't understand how that's possible," he retorted, examining the trout with a critical eye and giving the pan a gentle shake.

"Well, your hours do seem a bit erratic. And even if they were regular there doesn't seem to be a lot of potential customers up here."

"During the winter we get a very well-to-do ski crowd."

"Ah. I understand. It's a seasonal business."

"The gallery? A bit. Not that I let it affect my erratic business practices unduly. I get in my share of skiing!"

Kalinda shook her head. "Well, each to his own. You seem to live a very relaxed sort of lifestyle."

"Exactly. Just as you're supposed to do when you come up here. But you're not, are you?"

"Relaxed? At the moment I'm very comfortable," she countered firmly, taking another sip of the icy highball and preparing to parry his probing questions.

"Oh, you look the part, all right. Very cool and elegantly casual. But there's something about you that doesn't seem really relaxed. You're not nervous of me, by any chance?" he demanded interestedly.

"Of course not!" Her light laughter was genuine.

"You don't have to be so emphatic about it!" he growled wryly.

"Sorry," she mocked contritely. "I forgot about the ever-present male ego."

Rand shot her a quick, perusing glance as he hefted the pepper mill. "Tell me the truth," he grumbled humorously, "did you accept my offer of dinner because I represent a change of pace from your usual run of admirers?"

"Isn't that what a vacation is for? A change of pace?" she chuckled, enjoying the banter.

"I knew it," he groaned dramatically. "I'm fated to be a vacation fling!"

"Don't worry," Kalinda smiled. "Giving me dinner doesn't exactly put you into the category of a fling!"

"Good," he said smoothly. "Because we artistic types prefer to think in terms of *affairs,* not flings!"

Kalinda's gray eyes went a little cold. "I'm afraid having diner is not a prelude to an affair, either," she informed him quite firmly.

He watched her curiously for a moment, raising his own golden drink for a sip. "You don't like the idea of being the mistress of an artist-fisherman?"

"Not particularly!" The haughty tone was cool and definite.

"But all artists have mistresses. It's part of the mystique," he explained helpfully.

She let her budding annoyance show in her voice as Rand turned back to the trout. "Perhaps you can consider our association as a change of pace for yourself, then," she suggested deliberately.

"Yes, ma'am," he agreed humbly. Once again Kalinda felt a moment of unease. She had been quite certain since meeting Rand Alastair that she knew exactly what she was dealing with. But little things kept taking her by surprise. It was unsettling.

"Think of it as a case of two ships passing in the night," she advised blandly.

"A pity. I've been weaving artistic fantasies since I looked up and saw you scowling at me in the door of the shop," he grinned, reaching for plates on which to dish up the fish.

"Are you an artist?" she questioned, deciding it

was time to switch conversational topics. "Or do you just run the gallery?"

"I dabble," he admitted, setting the food on the redwood table and lifting the wine out of the chiller.

"In what?" she asked, getting out of the lounger and coming across to join him at the table. The combination of crisp salad, fresh trout, and grilled corn was whetting her appetite as no restaurant meal could have done.

"Pottery," he replied succinctly, taking his seat. "I did the piece you bought this afternoon."

"You did! Why didn't you say something? It's lovely! I adore art that serves a purpose," she confided. "I know that's not a proper approach, but I was born with this depressingly practical streak. I like things to be both functional and beautiful. I'm going to get a lot of use out of that bowl."

"Good," he said cheerfully. "I feel exactly the same way. Perhaps I'm more properly described as a craftsperson than an artist?"

"A meaningless distinction," Kalinda declared regally, going to work delicately on the trout. "Why should useful art be downgraded to a 'craft'?"

"My sentiments exactly," he smiled, looking quite pleased with himself. "I'll show you some of the other pieces I've done after dinner. That is, if you'd like to see them?"

She met his encouraging glance and smiled warmly. "Of course, I would."

A short, potent silence hung between them for an instant as they looked at each other. Kalinda found herself swallowing with a new twinge of uncertainty. What was wrong with her? She wasn't interested in this man except as a casual dinner date. Why this new restlessness which had begun to temporarily replace the nervousness she'd been experiencing? This new sensation had nothing at all to do with her plans for the coming weekend. The confrontation with David Hutton still awaited her. It should be the uppermost concern in her mind. Yet here she was being subtly overtaken by an altogether different mood.

Irritably she gave a mental shrug and made a deliberate effort to pull back from the spell she sensed her host was trying to weave. They were exactly what she'd described a few minutes earlier, two strangers who happened to encounter each other briefly but who shared nothing lasting or binding. A casual dinner engagement.

"I'll bet you're telling yourself I'm not your type," Rand murmured easily, taking a bite off the corn cob. He didn't appear concerned by his accurate guess.

"Why not?" she countered breezily. "If you're honest with yourself, you'd be saying the same thing. We are two very different kinds of people, aren't we, Rand?'' Firmly she tried to make him acknowledge that basic fact.

"Who can say? We've hardly gotten to know each other. Even if that were so, would it matter?''

"Oh, yes, it matters,'' she nodded.

"Meaning that you're much too practical to risk getting involved with a man who doesn't fit readily into your lifestyle?''

Kalinda decided it was time to take charge of the situation. Taking charge was something she did instinctively and well. "How long have you worked with pottery, Rand?''

He hesitated, as if trying to decide whether or not to let her change the topic. And then he lifted one smoothly muscled shoulder as if it wasn't all that important, after all.

"Nearly two years. I have a kiln in my workshop over there.'' He indicated a small building behind the house. "Are you sure you wouldn't rather talk about us?''

"Very sure,'' she smiled coolly.

"What can a host do except defer to the wishes of his guest?'' he whispered gallantly.

"Thank you,'' Kalinda retorted with the self-possession that comes from regularly having her wishes deferred to by others. "The trout is delicious.''

They lingered over dinner as the waning summer sun settled behind the mountain, casting the lake and its environs into shadows. The tall pine and fir among which the house nestled rustled lightly in the faint breeze and the bottle of Chardonnay slowly emptied. It was turning into a very pleasant evening, Kalinda decided, wondering how that could be when she had so much on her mind. But tonight Rand Alastair was making it possible for her to put her doubts and worries about the weekend aside for a while. She was grateful to him for it.

He displayed his pottery with an unaffected pleasure later after Kalinda had helped him clear the table and carry the dishes into the modern, compact kitchen. She went from piece to piece, genuinely admiring the warm colors, rich glazes, and original design.

"You're very talented," she remarked, carefully setting down the small pot she was holding and wondering privately how he could possibly make a living off the pottery and the gallery. She knew a lot about business, even if she didn't know a great deal about the specific business of running a small art and craft store.

"It's a hobby," he murmured as she turned around to face him. He was standing very close behind her, much closer than she had realized and Kalinda found herself swinging softly against his chest. His arms were around her even as she opened her lips to apologize. The impact sent a small shock through her and her gray eyes widened.

"I'm sorry," she managed, suddenly, fiercely aware of the warmth and strength in his lean, hard body. "I didn't realize you were standing so near…"

"My fault entirely," he assured her, his arms tightening around her, pulling her closer with a forcefulness she would have said earlier wasn't in character. "I've been looking for an excuse to kiss you all evening…."

Kalinda saw the lambent flame beginning to flare in the clear hazel gaze above her and wondered at her own reaction. It was curiosity, she decided, which was going to hold her still for his kiss. The same curiosity that had made her follow the sound of his voice that morning. There was something different about this man.

Before she had time to analyze the difference, Rand's mouth was covering her own.

Kalinda sensed the power in the arms which held her and knew with a rush of realism that, even if she hadn't been curious, she would still be standing in his embrace, awaiting his kiss. She knew in that moment that she couldn't have broken Rand's hold.

Two

Kalinda wasn't certain exactly what she was expecting from Rand's kiss, but it definitely wasn't the gentle, persuasive aggression she got. His kiss was a contradiction, she thought vaguely as her fingertips automatically came up to brace against the broad shoulders. Or was it? Could a man be both gentle and aggressive at the same time?

The warm, probing caress grew around her, enveloping her senses even as she tried to retain some control over herself and him. It was like stepping into an inviting pool of water only to discover silvery quicksand beneath one's feet.

"There's cool silk on the surface," he husked against her lips. "But I have a hunger to find out what's underneath..."

"Rand, please, I..." Kalinda's small effort to halt the soft invasion collapsed as his tongue parted her lips.

She heard him groan, felt his hands slide down the bare silk dress to her waist and was unable to repress the little shiver of excitement that coursed through her.

Her mouth yielded to the heated challenge with a will of its own. Rand's tongue explored the sweet, intimate interior as a jungle cat seeks out a forest den. His lips moved on hers, forcing a dampening, electric contact that denied any attempt at retreat on her part.

Kalinda grew a little shocked at her own response. This wasn't like her, as any of her recent escorts could have testified! Even with David it hadn't been this sudden, this overwhelming....

Rand's fingers dipped lower, shaping the curve of her waist, pressing with growing urgency into the flare of her hips. He pulled her abruptly closer, nestling her into the cradle of his thighs and Kalinda sucked in her breath on a low moan of surprise mingled with dismay.

"Don't be afraid of me," he growled coaxingly. "I won't hurt you." His hands moved on her, sliding along the thin silk and leaving a trail of warmth on hips and thighs and waist. He felt her tremble and she heard his sigh of pleasure.

"We've been building toward this from the moment we met,'' he whispered, seeking the edge of her mouth with his lips and then beginning to track the line of her cheek to the corner of her closed eyes. ''I spent all afternoon thinking about taking you in my arms.''

''I...I hope you didn't shut the gallery again on my account!'' she managed a little shakily. She wasn't surprised to hear him admit he'd wanted to kiss her from the start. She was old enough to know men often reacted quickly to a woman who caught their fancy. It was her own appallingly swift reaction that alarmed her. The moment she'd felt his arms go around her she'd known a strange kind of longing. And that was definitely not normal for her!

''Had to,'' he muttered on a laughing groan. ''How could I work when all I could think about was feeding you and plying you with liquor?''

''Oh, Rand, this is ridiculous!''

''No,'' he countered thickly, the tip of his tongue dancing lightly in and around her ear, ''this is desire. I told you I needed a mistress...''

''Then you'll have to keep interviewing bored lady tourists,'' she flung back with a trace of acid in her voice. ''The trout was delicious but it was only worth a good-night kiss, not a night in bed!''

''Ah, well,'' he murmured philosophically, ''I shall have to be satisfied with what I can get.''

He lifted one hand and slipped off the small, gold earring she wore in her left ear. He dropped the earring into his pocket as his teeth closed teasingly, temptingly where the piece of jewelry had been.

It was a small, seemingly insignificant action, yet when he repeated it with the other ear, Kalinda began to feel as if he were stripping her of her very clothing.

She made an attempt to pull away from the growing spell of seduction, easing her head back out of reach and pushing firmly against him. But he only took advantage of the position to bury his lips against her throat. The next shiver that shook Kalinda was almost frightening in its intensity.

His hands stroked up her waist with slow, caressing movements until they rested just under the weight of her breasts. When she twisted slightly to escape the intimate touch she knew would come next, Kalinda somehow found her nipple caught under the palm of his hand. Through the material of the silk and the scrap of lacy bra her body reacted without her volition, the nipple hardening.

In spite of her resolve to keep the embrace from going any further, Kalinda's nails bit convulsively into the fabric of the pin-stripe shirt, seeking the feel of the muscled flesh underneath.

"Silk and flame," he muttered, his voice deepening as he felt her response. "Where have you been hiding yourself, honey? Think of all the nights we've missed!"

"Just as we're going to miss this one," she retorted a little grimly, conscious of the catch in her words. "I'm not going to bed with you, Rand."

"Tell me that again in a few minutes," he advised and moved, sweeping her up into his arms before she realized his intention.

Her arm circled his neck in an instinctive gesture against falling although he held her with a rocklike security.

"I won't be carried off to bed, Rand," Kalinda snapped arrogantly, unaccustomed to having her dinner dates proceed against her declared wishes. She still didn't believe herself to be in trouble but there was no doubt matters were in danger of getting out of hand.

"The couch?" he suggested hopefully, the laughing gleam in his eyes somehow adding to, rather than subtracting from the desire she saw there.

He strode across the cream carpet to the long caramel couch and settled her gently down on it. When Kalinda opened her eyes after the ensuing moment of vertigo, she found him descending on top of her and her words of determined protest were muffled in her throat as she caught her breath against his weight.

"Damn it, I will not let you…"

"Just let me kiss you," he begged huskily, dropping tiny, featherlight caresses on her cheeks, her eyelids, her ears. When his mouth returned to hers his hand simultaneously moved once more to cover her small breast. The twin assault shocked her senses, causing her to writhe beneath him.

Instantly he responded by crushing her hips intimately with his own, forcing her into the deep cushions until she cried out in growing passion.

"Flame for me, Lady Silk," he growled urgently, nipping her bare shoulder with his teeth and then soothing the scented area with his tongue. "I want to see you go up in flames for me tonight!"

The soft material of the dress began to fall away from her and Kalinda realized dimly he had found the delicate fastenings. She knew she ought to stop him but she couldn't seem to say the words. A passionate curiosity was driving her now and when she felt him undo the front clasp of the small bra she wound her fingers deeply into the chestnut hair with a breathless moan.

"Oh, please! Please..."

"I will," he promised hoarsely, "I will!"

Rand bent his head to find the tips of her breasts with undisguised male need, his tongue curling around the taut nipples as his fingers traced patterns down her bare stomach.

Ahead of his questing hand, the silk dress continued to give way until Kalinda knew the touch of his fingers just inside the edge of her satiny briefs.

She gasped violently and her own hands worked

their way inside the collar of his shirt. He moved under her touch the way a cat moves under stroking fingers. She found his uninhibited response deeply, incredibly arousing and without further thought she sought the buttons of the shirt.

A moment later they both lay naked from the waist up, the curling cloud of chestnut hair on Rand's chest exciting and sensual on Kalinda's softness.

Her breath was coming more quickly now and common sense was a rapidly deteriorating commodity. She arched beneath him and he used his strength to tease her by crushing her gently until she couldn't move. Somehow the restraint only served to excite her all the more and Kalinda felt the driving need surge through her body.

It wasn't until she felt him part her legs with his own and knew the hardening maleness of him even through the fabric of the trousers he still wore that some semblance of rational thought returned.

"Rand...Rand, please. That's enough! I never meant..."

"It's all right," he soothed, holding her still as she began to struggle beneath him. "Just let it happen. It's going to be so good, honey. I want you so badly tonight."

Kalinda moved her head restlessly on the cushion, the sleek knot of her hair long since undone and floating around her. She heard the inevitable

words, *I want you,* and they reinforced her efforts
to regain control of herself and the situation.

"I'm sorry," she whispered, conscious of her
own part in the matter. "I didn't mean for things
to go this far!" Carefully she began to push against
his bare shoulders, her nails digging into the
bronzed skin.

"Kalinda!" His desire-deepened voice cracked
slightly as he lifted his head to stare down at her.
"What's wrong? Stop fighting it, sweetheart. You
want this as much as I do!"

She shook her head in denial, well aware of the
want in him. She had to deal with this very cautiously. She had allowed him to become thoroughly
aroused and she knew so little about him! How did
she know what to expect when he finally realized
she meant to call everything to a halt?

For all she knew he might turn violent. God!
How had she managed to get herself into this?

"Rand, please," she begged gently, straining
away from his hardness, "I want to stop. I never
intended for things to go this far. Please let me
go...."

For an instant the hazel eyes flashed almost green
and she knew a momentary fear. And then the frustrated, angry male glitter was gone to be replaced
by a cold, masculine restraint. It was only when
that, too, disappeared to reveal rueful dismay that
Kalinda knew she could relax.

"You're serious, aren't you?" Rand muttered dryly.

"Yes, I…I never intended for this to happen tonight. Believe me!"

"I believe you! But you see, I fully intended for it to happen!"

"Rand, that's idiotic," Kalinda scolded bracingly, aware of her nakedness and the weight of his body. "You hardly know me!"

"I wanted you the minute I saw you," he told her succinctly, his hands framing her face between rough palms. "I'm more than happy to be a vacation fling for you, Kalinda Brady," he murmured enticingly.

"Thanks a lot! Very generous of you. But it so happens, I'm not interested in that sort of relationship!"

"How about the affair we discussed earlier?" he whispered seductively, his thumbs making probing circles at the corners of her mouth.

"Out of the question!" she snapped, beginning to grow angry. "Let me up, Rand, it's time I went back to the motel."

"Calm down, I'll take you back if that's what you really want.…"

"It is!"

"On one condition," he concluded a little too gently.

She glared up at him. "What condition?"

"That I can see you tomorrow."

Kalinda grabbed a deep breath. "I don't see why you should want that. I can guarantee I won't feel any differently tomorrow!"

"How can you be sure of that? I'll have all day to convince you," he reminded her, his mouth quirking in amused promise. "Who knows how you'll feel by this time tomorrow night?"

"I know what I want and what I don't want."

He hesitated and then said with unexpected coolness, "Yes, I've gathered that. Which brings up a very interesting point."

"What are you talking about?"

"You do seem like the sort of woman who makes up her own mind and does what she wishes most of the time."

Kalinda eyes him narrowly, wondering where this was leading. "I am."

"Then what are you doing here?" he countered swiftly.

"Here? I told you. I had nothing else to do this evening and the trout sounded good...."

"That's not what I mean and you know it. I find myself curious as to what you're doing here in our little mountain retreat. It's obvious you're bored and you're not the sort who likes to head for a rustic environment when you feel like getting away from it all."

"How do you know that?" she retorted, alarmed.

"As I've already pointed out, you barely know me!"

"I happen to be a very good judge of character," he drawled. "And, honey, as delightful as you look at this moment, I have to say you did seem a little out of place today wandering around town in your hundred-dollar shirt and those designer slacks!"

Kalinda felt herself go red under his mocking gaze and tried to free her hands in order to cover her naked breasts. But he ignored the effort and waited for a reply!

"My reasons for being here are personal," she muttered with all the arrogance she could command under the circumstances.

He smiled dangerously. "I deduced that much. How personal?"

"I do not intend to discuss that."

"You really are used to giving orders, aren't you?" he observed wonderingly.

"I am, but you don't appear to be very good at taking them," she shot back grittily. "Will you please let me up?"

He didn't move for a moment and Kalinda found herself holding her breath as he studied her.

"If you'll grant my condition," he finally agreed with a short nod.

She sighed. "I'll have lunch with you tomorrow if you're sure you want to see me again." At least he was off the other topic!

He sat up almost at once and Kalinda could almost hear the belated *click* as her brain finally found the right gear. She sat absorbing the impact of his hard profile as he buttoned his shirt and then she moved her head in a wry gesture of self-disgust.

"You did that deliberately, didn't you?" There was a trace of unwilling admiration in her voice. Kalinda was businesswoman enough to recognize innate manipulative talent when she came across it. This man really had wasted his life out here in the wilderness!

"Did what?" he asked innocently, adjusting the collar of his shirt as he slanted her an intriguing glance.

She waved a hand. "You know. First you bring up your real goal, which is to see me tomorrow. When I don't leap at that, you bring up another matter about which I feel very strongly."

"The little issue of what you're doing here in the mountains in the first place?" he clarified helpfully.

She nodded. "And then, when you have me thoroughly ruffled on that subject, you reintroduce the main goal. By that time it seems easier to agree to it so that I can get you to leave me alone on the second topic!"

"You're very perceptive," he grinned engagingly.

"And you're very good at manipulating people,"

she grumbled dryly. "Now it's my turn to ask some questions."

"Go ahead," he invited cheerfully, sinking back into a corner of the caramel-colored couch and regarding her with lazy invitation.

"Why are you so set on seeing me tomorrow? You're not going to find yourself in bed with me tomorrow night, I can guarantee!"

"Can you?"

"Definitely! I have no interest in a fling with you or anyone else, Rand," she retorted steadily.

"I understand," he astonished her by saying softly.

"Then why...?"

"I still want to see you, Kalinda. I'm attracted to you. I was the moment I saw you. It sometimes happens like that, you know."

"For a man."

He said nothing, not denying the small accusation. There was a waiting silence and then Kalinda went on carefully, "Could it be you're a little bored, yourself?"

He blinked, the coppery lashes brushing the rugged cheekbones for an instant and then he regarded her with his clear gaze. "Why should I be bored? I have the gallery, the pottery, my fishing and I'm living in the heart of God's county. And there are a few women around, you know," he added placidly. "I mean, besides yourself!"

She flushed, looking away. "I'm sure there are!"

"So what makes you think I'm pursuing you out of sheer boredom?"

"Forget it." She got to her feet. "I was just making an observation. You're obviously content with your niche in life or you wouldn't be here, would you?"

"No."

She forced a smile. "So I was wrong in my observation, just as you're wrong if you think you're going to talk me into a fling or a short-term affair. Now it's time you took me back to the motel. The dinner was delightful."

He ranged easily to his feet, his gleaming eyes never leaving her still-flushed features. "About your personal reasons for being in my mountains…"

She smiled brilliantly. "I'm ready to leave, Rand."

He gave her a mocking bow. "I'm at my Lady's command. The Lotus awaits."

But she should have known he wouldn't give up that easily, Kalinda told herself the next day as she lounged beside him on a picnic blanket by the lake. Rand Alastair wasn't the sort of man to surrender so simply and easily. She knew that much about him even though he still confused her in many ways.

Added to her own growing restlessness and nervousness, his delicate probing was going to send her over the edge, she decided midway through the delicious lunch he had packed.

"How long will you be staying here, Kalinda?"

She munched the cheddar sandwich in her hand with relish. "A couple more days," she said cautiously.

He was stretched out beside her, wearing his jeans again and an open-necked sport shirt which revealed the tanned, sinewy length of his arms. The chestnut hair was lightly tousled by the breeze off the lake and his eyes were half-closed against the dancing sunlight. Kalinda was suddenly forced to acknowledge to herself that he seemed very attractive to her.

She directed her attention toward the opposite shore of the lake, feeling his hooded gaze on her. She had pushed up the sleeves of her button-necked tunic top which she wore over a pair of white pants and kicked off her sandals. Kalinda felt relaxed on one level, but wary on another. The lunch had been enjoyable but it hadn't taken her long to realize Rand was hot on the trail he had scented last night. His curiosity was aroused, she supposed. Just as hers was about him.

"You're not sure exactly how many days you'll be here?"

"I expect I'll be leaving the day after tomorrow."

"Why so soon?" he pressed.

"I have a business to run, remember?"

"Isn't the boss entitled to a vacation?" he smiled knowingly.

"Of course. This isn't it, though." As he'd already clearly guessed. There was not much point in pretending she was here for her annual holiday, Kalinda had decided early in the game. Damn the man's persistence! But she had only herself to blame, she admitted grimly. She had wanted to see him again today, even knowing what to expect.

"Ah, yes. The personal business which brings you to our neck of the woods. It will all be over within a couple of days?"

"Yes. Now, if you don't mind, I'd rather talk about something else."

"Fishing?"

She laughed. "Hardly!"

"My plans for us tomorrow night?" he suggested hopefully.

Her laughter died at once. "I'm afraid that's out of the question, Rand. I won't be seeing you tomorrow night."

He went very still beside her and she bit her lip in vexation. But it was the truth and there was no sense letting him think she would be free tomorrow night.

"Tonight's our last evening together?" he asked quietly.

"Yes."

"But you'll be here in town tomorrow night?"

She said nothing. Why was she letting him push her like this? It couldn't be that subconsciously she *wanted* to tell him the truth, could it? That she needed to talk to someone? She had always been so self-possessed, so confident. But she had doubts about what was going to happen tomorrow night when she confronted David. She'd had doubts all along. And that wasn't like her.

"So that's it," he growled softly.

"What?" She swung her neat head around to look at him, saw the cool fire in his eyes and wished she hadn't taken her gaze off the lake. She felt abruptly trapped by the power in him.

"You're here to meet a man." The words dropped like stones out on the lake.

Kalinda didn't move. "It's business," she finally said coldly, struggling to break the bonds he'd placed on her. "Personal, private business."

"You're not looking for a fling with me because you're here to have an affair with another man."

"Rand! Stop it! You know nothing about the matter!" Dear Lord! What was wrong with her to have let him guess so close to the mark? She must be crazy! Or secretly desperate to talk it over with someone, she added grimly to herself.

"Don't you think it might be just a tad dangerous to amuse yourself with me while you wait for Mr.

Wonderful to arrive? What if he hits town early and finds you've spent the time flirting with a local shopkeeper?''

''Of all the ridiculous things to say! I am not flirting with you!''

''I'd call it flirting if I arrived at a rendezvous and found my woman had spent a couple of evenings with another man while waiting for me to show up!'' he rasped bitterly. ''And what happened on my couch last night definitely does not come under the category of casual acquaintance!''

She realized he was angry, furiously so.

''That's the only category it could come under,'' she grated feelingly. ''All we have is a casual acquaintance!''

''If that's how you treat your fleeting relationships, I'd like to see what happens after you've known a man a couple of weeks!''

She flinched, pulling her eyes away from his condemning glare. He still hadn't shifted from the sprawled position he'd taken, one jeaned leg drawn up as he rested on his elbow. Nevertheless, she had the distinct impression he was sorely tempted to wrap his fingers around her throat. Could she blame him?

''I'm not here to have an affair with anyone,'' she muttered, setting down the remains of her sandwich as her appetite vanished. She couldn't meet his eyes at all now.

"But you're meeting a man tomorrow night?" he prodded tightly.

Kalinda said nothing, letting her own silence tell the tale.

"Want to tell me about it?"

That brought her head back around with a snap to stare in astonishment. The wholly new tone in his dark voice took her completely by surprise. She had been prepared for belligerence; male outrage at her callous treatment of him, perhaps. But she certainly hadn't been expecting this sudden, soothing, calming offer! Where was the anger he'd been holding in check?

"You can, you know," he went on, mouth twisted beguilingly. "You can tell me the whole story."

"How do you know there's a story to tell?" she challenged carefully, uncertain of her own weakening reaction.

"Instinct. I know it sounds ridiculous, but I really do have fairly sound instincts about people and what makes them tick."

"I know," she whispered. "You're also good at using that knowledge to manipulate people!"

The edge of his mouth hardened. "You don't seem to lack much in the way of perception, yourself!"

"I've learned to recognize a few things," she half-smiled dismissingly. "But I've had on-the-job training in the business world. With you I think it must be instinctive, just as you said. Something you were born with!''

''Are you going to tell me about tomorrow night?''

''I'm not sure. The fact that I've let you push me this close to the subject makes me think I might,'' she said quite honestly. ''But if I do, I shall probably be killing my chance at another trout dinner tonight!'' She managed the last with an almost sad flippancy.

''It's steak this evening, not trout,'' he quipped. ''And I promise I won't rescind the offer.''

''Even if I admit I'm here to meet a man?'' she dared softly.

''I already know that much.''

She waited before saying very coolly, very remotely, ''You're not going to talk me out of it, you know. I've come this far, I'm going to go through with it.''

''That remains to be seen.''

Kalinda rested her arms on her drawn-up knees and shook her head with grave determination. ''No one could talk me out of it at this stage. A woman seldom gets this kind of opportunity. I'd be a fool to throw it away.''

''Exactly what sort of opportunity are we talking about, Kalinda?'' he demanded in a low voice that betrayed nothing of his feelings.

"Revenge," she said simply.

"Revenge!"

He sat up, reaching out to catch her chin and force her around to face him. "My God! You really mean it, don't you?" he breathed, searching her intent, determined features. "Who is this man you're going to have your revenge on, Kalinda Brady?"

"My ex-fiancé." The words sounded stark, even to her own ears. "He dropped me two years ago when my father was killed and it was discovered the firm was in bad shape. David Hutton, it turned out, was marrying me because he wanted my father's company."

"And now he wants you back?"

Kalinda smiled grimly. "I've let him think I'm interested. I've agreed to meet him up here for the sake of what we once had, as they say."

"Why did you agree to rendezvous here? Why not Denver?"

"Oh, we couldn't do that," she explained acidly. "David's married now, you see."

"You little fool," he breathed. "You crazy little fool. Exactly what are you going to do tomorrow night when he shows up expecting you to throw yourself into his arms?"

"I'm going to throw his offer in his face, naturally. I'm going to let David Hutton beg me for another chance, listen to him offer to divorce his wife, and then I'm going to laugh and tell him exactly what I think of him! The one thing David can't stand is to be laughed at.''

Three

Rand stared at her for a long, taut moment, his expression hard and unreadable.

"You can't go through with it," he finally said flatly. "It's too damn dangerous."

"Dangerous!" Kalinda almost smiled at that. "David's not the physical type. He wouldn't..."

"Rape you? Don't be a fool. Any man could be dangerous in a situation such as you're planning! And you've already misjudged him once, haven't you?"

She winced at his pointed comment. "That was two years ago. I've learned a lot since then. I know him for what he is."

He shook his head. "What makes you think that?"

"I learned everything I needed to know about the man when he came to me after my father's funeral and said he was breaking off the engagement!"

"All you learned at that point was that he'd wanted to marry you in order to gain control of what he'd assumed was a successful company. You discovered he was no longer interested in you or the company when its financial status had been revealed. But you didn't learn anything about what he'd be likely to do in a confrontation such as the one you're planning!" Rand's voice was chilling. "Face it, he might very well turn vicious. But that's not the only risk you're running!"

She frowned, wishing on the one hand she'd never let him discover her real reasons for being in town and knowing on the other that some part of her had wanted to talk to another human being about the reckless plan. Why had that convenient human being turned out to be this unsympathetic male?

"What other risk could there be?" she snapped, goaded by his glowering disapproval.

"Are you sure revenge is the real reason you're planning this?" he growled. "Two years ago you were in love with the man. Maybe you're really here to see if you can pick up the pieces...."

"No!" The idea was ludicrous! "After what he did to me?"

"He hurt you. People hurt other people all the

time but that doesn't always kill the love they have for each other.''

''I assure you a healthy dose of reality killed any feeling I might have had for David Hutton two years ago,'' she blazed.

''You still feel strongly enough about the man to want revenge,'' he reminded her coolly. ''They say hate is akin to love.''

''That's absurd and you know it,'' she scoffed with great certainty. Whatever else she felt for David Hutton after two years, Kalinda knew love had nothing to do with her emotions.

''Exactly what did happen two years ago after David took back his ring?'' Rand regarded her probingly, sounding as if he were trying to get to the bottom of a serious mystery.

Kalinda lifted one shoulder casually. ''I had my hands full trying to salvage the business. I didn't spend a lot of time brooding over my tragic romance, if that's what you're thinking.''

''Brady Data Processing, I take it, is no longer on the skids?'' he murmured dryly.

''No, it's not.'' That remark brought an unconscious smile of pride and satisfaction to Kalinda's lips. ''We're on the way back. We've shown profits for the last three quarters, in fact.''

One chestnut eyebrow lifted in acknowledgment of the accomplishment. ''You must have worked hard during the past two years.''

"I did," she admitted simply. It was the truth. She had literally buried herself in her work. And now, finally, it had all begun to pay off. She could afford to relax and enjoy her well-earned success.

"Why?" he asked evenly.

She hesitated. "I had to."

"In order to forget Hutton?" he demanded, sounding thoroughly irritated at that possibility.

She shook her head, her mouth quirking upward. "It had nothing to do with David. I had to try to salvage the company because so many people were depending on me. You don't know what it was like."

"An old, established family firm with employees and members of the board who'd started out with your father while still in their teens?" he hazarded dryly. "People who'd spent their whole working lives there?"

She looked at him in astonishment. "How did you know?"

"I told you, we aren't totally isolated up here," he retorted cryptically. "I've heard of companies like your father's. So bound by traditional ways of doing things that they gently begin to sink beneath the waves of progress. Is that what was happening at the time your father was killed?"

"I'm afraid so. After I got my degree in business administration I went to work for another company. I knew I wouldn't fit in at my father's firm. Then he was killed and the board of directors asked me to consider taking over the day-to-day management. After all, I'd inherited it and them along with all those long-time employees. It was almost feudal!''

''And you didn't have the heart to liquidate or sell out?''

''How could I do that to all those people? But after a few months I realized there was more to it than just a sense of responsibility....''

''It became a challenge?'' he murmured.

''As I've said before, you're very perceptive,'' Kalinda smiled.

''So now, two years later, you've got the company back on its feet and David Hutton is trying to slip back into your life. Doesn't that strike you as something of a coincidence?''

Kalinda stared at him, shocked at that line of reasoning and then shook her head firmly. ''David is thoroughly involved with his own firm; the manufacturing business where he was vice-president at the time of my father's death has moved him up to president. Why should he be interested in Brady Data Processing now?''

There was a lengthy silence from Rand's side of the picnic blanket.

''Simple greed?'' he finally suggested caustically.

She thought about that, wryly admitting that finding out David's renewed interest in her was once again based on Brady Data Processing would be a blow to her ego.

"He married well. Very well. He's running a successful business."

"All of which might make him more greedy than ever."

"Where did you gain all this vast insight into the motivations of other people?" she grumbled. "You must meet quite a wide variety of tourists up here!"

"I do."

"Well, what you've just suggested only makes me more determined than ever to go through with my plan. If I'm right I'll have the satisfaction of denying him me. If you're right, I'll have the satisfaction of denying him the firm!"

"Neither of which is an adequate reason for taking the risk of seeing him again, dammit! You could get hurt in more ways than one, can't you get that through your head? What's the matter? Hasn't there been any other man in the past two years who could take your mind off him?"

Kalinda gave him a startled, too-revealing glance and he nodded in grim satisfaction. "So that's it. He's the last man you were serious about. You've spent the past two years devoting your energies to your firm and you haven't had time for a proper, flaming romance which might have dimmed the memory of your ex-fiancé!"

"That's a crazy line of logic! And here I was

thinking you so perceptive!'' she hissed, infuriated with him suddenly.

"What you need is someone to replace the memories with a much more interesting reality." Rand reached for her as Kalinda, seeing the flicker of intent in his eyes, started to edge away. But she wasn't quick enough.

"Rand, don't..."

"Give me one night, Kalinda," he grated, his hands on her shoulders. "Just one night..."

"Why, you egotistical fool! What makes you think one night with a vacation *fling* would be enough to wipe out the memories of another man? How dare you even suggest..."

Her words were choked off as she was pressed back onto the blanket. Rand moved swiftly, anchoring her twisting legs with his thigh and catching her wrists in one of his callus-roughened hands. Memories poured through her at his determined touch, but the memories were of the previous evening, not two years ago.

"You weren't thinking of Hutton last night, were you?" he challenged, holding her still beneath him, his hazel eyes gleaming with purpose and the beginnings of desire. "And somehow, I get the feeling you're not thinking of his kisses right now either!"

"Rand, listen to me," Kalinda pleaded, knowing she was not exactly in a position to goad him further. She would have to use reason and the truth if she wanted to calm him. "I'm not carrying a torch for David Hutton. I'm angry at him for what he did to me two years ago, but I'm not still in love with him! Believe me! I just want a chance to pay him back for treating me so shabbily. It's called poetic justice!"

"It's called being stupid," he retorted, leaning his weight across her chest and gently crushing her breasts beneath the thin covering of the tunic top. With his free hand he lightly stroked the line of her throat. Kalinda felt the slight tremor of response in her body and knew he'd felt it, too.

"I can assure you that calling me stupid is not a good method of seducing me!"

His fingers trailed to the unbuttoned collar of the tunic and he smiled crookedly. "Who knows? Perhaps lady executives respond to the more unusual methods!"

"Let me go, Rand," she ordered forcefully, her eyes narrowed as she looked up at him from the vulnerable position.

His face softened and she heard the new, coaxing note in his voice. "Honey, can't you see you're on the verge of making a gigantic mistake? You've said I'm perceptive. Why don't you pay more attention to that perception? Regardless of your motivations, the risks are too great. In addition to being perceptive, I'm also a man. Give me some credit for being able to predict how another man might react in the situation you're trying to set up?''

"How would you react?" she whispered, eyes widening with the question. She didn't know what had made her ask it. Overhead the pines swayed, breaking the path of sunlight so that it dappled their bodies. Kalinda was violently aware of the warm strength of Rand and the way his maleness seemed a part of their wild surroundings. The clean, musky scent of him reached her nostrils with a tantalizing tang that elicited a response from her body.

"That's not easy to answer," he confessed a little roughly, "because I can't conceive of ever letting you go in the first place."

"Of course you can," she scoffed bitterly. "I'll bet you're an old hand at managing the short-term affair!"

"If I did find myself in Hutton's shoes for whatever reason," he went on deliberately, ignoring her provocation, "I doubt I'd meekly sit back and let you have your revenge. If I'd arrived at an isolated mountain resort expecting to rekindle an old romance, I'd make damn sure something did, indeed, get ignited. You'd wind up in my bed, Kalinda, regardless of your intentions."

"But you're not David!" she shot back warily.

"No, I'm not Hutton," he agreed deeply and lowered his head to take her lips with a passion that Kalinda forced herself to admit she'd wanted to taste again. Ever since he'd first exposed her to it last night.

His mouth moved on hers with mounting desire as his hand slid down the buttons of the tunic, unfastening each in turn. When his fingers found her unconfined breasts, Kalinda gasped, the soft, broken moan in her throat stifled by his probing tongue.

Her own tongue moved instinctively to engage in the small, intimate duel with his and her arms circled him. She raked her nails almost tenderly down the back of his neck and under his collar, delighting once more in the reflexive arching of his body against her.

"Kalinda, Kalinda," he groaned as he slid his leg between hers. "Give me one night. Just one night. I swear you'll forget all about him by morning!"

He reached down to push her legs farther apart, letting his hand trace an erotic pattern against the material of her white pants. She sucked in her breath as he wove the pattern steadily upward along her inner thigh. His mouth began to explore the line of her throat, moving slowly, inevitably toward the hardening peak of her breast.

"Oh, Rand, Rand," she cried softly, "I shouldn't let you do this to me. I know I shouldn't. It's crazy..."

"Stop worrying about it and just accept the way things are between us," he murmured against the warmth of her skin. "There's nothing wrong with two people getting very lucky unexpectedly."

Before she could summon her thoughts for a rational protest, his teeth had closed carefully on one nipple, sending electric waves through her. The seductive hand traveling along her thigh reached the warm juncture of her legs and she closed her eyes tightly, knowing he must be aware of the heat he was generating in her.

"Honey, you're practically melting in my hands," he breathed with beguiling satisfaction as his fingers closed briefly over the feminine heart of her desire. "Don't you realize I must have all of you? I have to know what it's like to lose myself completely in your body. I've never ached so badly for a woman in my life!"

Kalinda writhed, arching herself against his hand and felt the instant response of his own body. Trembling, she began a sensitive, questing path down his side until she reached the barrier of his jeans. Restlessly, deliciously, she slipped her fingers just inside and heard his hoarse reaction.

"Please touch me," Rand begged, even as he began to fumble with the clasp of her white trousers. "I need to feel your hands on me. So soft, so exciting."

Unable to resist the urgent demand in him, Kalinda slowly undid the fastening of his jeans. She felt the trembling in him and knew a womanly

power she had never before known. It was somehow very important and wholly satisfying to know
she could make this one particular man respond. As
her senses whirled dizzily some vague instinct told
her that this was the only man in the world whose
response counted.

With delicate, tender caresses she explored the
hard, fully aroused male frame. He reacted to the
buttery touches as if they were glowing lasers.
When she sank her fingers into the muscular but-
tock, she heard him call out her name with a fierce-
ness that excited her beyond reason.

But even as she sought to inflame him further,
Kalinda was slipping rapidly under the spell Rand
was working on her own body. She felt the possessive spread of his fingers on her stomach and turned
her head into his shoulder with a sigh of need when
his hand went lower.

"You can't respond like this to me and still be
thinking of that other man," Rand groaned huskily,
his mouth on the silky skin of her stomach. "You
can't! I won't let you!"

"No," she whispered brokenly. "I'm only thinking of you. I can barely think at all!"

"That's the way it should be. Lose yourself in
me, sweetheart, just as I'm losing myself in you."

Kalinda felt the waves of desire wash over her,
knew a surging excitement she'd never experienced
and slowly common sense fell aside.

With a deep sound of pleasure and anticipation, Rand moved, rolling onto his back and pulling Kalinda down across his chest. She blinked as her equilibrium swam momentarily and then reacted to the hot invitation in his eyes.

Dropping passionate little kisses along his shoulder, Kalinda pushed aside the sport shirt Rand wore. Recklessly she wound her fingers in the hair on his chest, tugging gently.

"Vixen," he muttered enticingly and tightened his grasp on her hip until she gasped from the curious pleasure-pain.

"You're a menace to the male of the species, do you realize that?" he charged on a husky note of impassioned laughter.

"No," she denied vehemently, her light-colored hair falling loose to swirl across his chest as she dipped her tongue into the pit of his firm stomach. "I'm not normally like this," she added uncomprehendingly. "I've never felt quite like this. You do something crazy to me, Rand Alastair."

His hold on her became at once soothing and even more demanding as he heard the honest bewilderment in her words.

"The feeling," he growled, "is mutual. My God, woman! To think we could have gone for the rest of our lives not knowing this sensation! If nothing else, I shall have to be grateful to Hutton for luring you up here!"

Kalinda froze. David's name was like a dash of cold water in her face. Slowly, with a gathering sense of amazed confusion, she lifted her head. What was she doing? This was utterly insane! She hardly knew this man and here she was making love to him as if he were a lover of long-standing!

Mutely she met his eyes, knowing he was at once aware of the self-disgust in her own bleak gaze.

"Kalinda?" he whispered pleadingly. "What's wrong, sweetheart?" His hands encircled her waist, holding her in place above him. "Stop looking at me like that. I'm not going to hurt you."

"I...know," she managed, struggling to bring her reeling senses back under control. "But I never meant... I didn't mean to get involved like this again today. I don't understand what you do to me, but it's all wrong! We're all wrong. We...we don't belong together...."

Painfully, she tried to separate herself from him, thrusting a hand through her hair to sweep it back from her face. She sat up with the greatest care, as if the movement was incredibly difficult. His eyes never left hers and she saw dismay and a growing coolness begin to wipe out the passion that had looked out at her from the hazel depths.

"Damn it to hell," he muttered, his hands still on her waist. "It was Hutton's name that did it, wasn't it? What a fool I am. You'd think a man would know when to keep his mouth shut!"

In spite of the charged atmosphere, Kalinda knew a rueful spark of humor as she listened to him condemn his own stupidity. "I'm sorry, Rand. I should never have let things go this far. I honestly don't know what got into me."

He regarded her with a narrowed, seething glance. "You've been a chief executive officer for so long you automatically accept the responsibility for whatever happens around you or to you, right? I've got news for you, darling, I was involved in this, too! In fact, I started it!"

He sat up, releasing her to rake his hand impatiently through his thick, tousled hair. "And it's all my fault it's ground to a premature halt!"

"For which I'm very grateful," she flung back, stung by his scathing tone. "I have no intention of being a one-night stand for you, dammit!"

"And I have no intention of letting you be a one-night stand for your ex-fiancé!"

"How many times do I have to tell you, that's not the way it's going to be? I'll be in charge tomorrow night and I know exactly what I'm doing!"

"The hell you do! You're so blinded by your memories of that bastard you can't see the stupidity of your own plans! If you ran Brady Data Processing with that degree of insanity, you would have lost it to bankruptcy long ago!"

"What do you know about running a company into insolvency?" she gritted tersely. "Don't talk

to me about how to run my life or my business. We
live in two separate worlds and you aren't in any
position to give me advice!'' She leaped to her feet,
madly straightening her clothing and frantically trying not to cry. Why the threat of tears? She wished
desperately she could figure out why this man had
such an incredible effect on her. It made no sense
at all!

He stood up beside her with a quick glance and
caught her wrist.

"Kalinda, I'm sorry," he muttered. "Please believe me. I never meant to shout at you like that.
But it's so damn frustrating...."

"A man your age must know how to handle a
little masculine frustration by now!"

"I'm not talking about the way you just frustrated me physically," he rasped, giving her a small
shake. "I'm talking about how frustrating it is to
try to make you see reason. You can't go through
with your plans for tomorrow night. It's too dangerous." His voice lowered gruffly, persuasively.
"Please give me a chance to make you change your
mind. I meant what I said a little while ago. Give
me one night and I can make you forget him."

"Your ego is as vast as David's!"

The moment the words left her mouth Kalinda
could have bitten her tongue. Red stained the
tanned heights of his cheekbones as he reacted to
the comparison of himself with the other man. His
fingers on her wrist tightened bruisingly.

Impulsively, without stopping to think, Kalinda lifted her hand to touch the side of his face with a placating gesture, her eyes soft and apologetic.

"I'm sorry I said that," she whispered huskily. "I didn't mean to imply you were anything like him. I know you're not, believe me."

She waited in an agony of suspense, watching the play of emotions across his features. She hadn't meant to hurt him, hadn't really stopped to think that he could be hurt. Not by her. He hardly knew her!

"That," he finally said evenly, "was a rather low blow!"

She winced, unconsciously sinking her teeth into her lower lip as she met his hard, accusing stare.

"I know. I'm sorry." She didn't know what else to say.

He searched her face a moment longer and then appeared to relax slightly. "But maybe you weren't so far off the mark," he sighed. "I suppose it must sound like sheer male ego talking when I tell you all I need is one night to put that man out of your head forever."

Kalinda said nothing, but she didn't deny his statement. His mouth twisted wryly. He raised his free hand and wrapped it around her neck under the fall of brown-blond hair. She felt him lightly massaging her nape and against her will her knees seemed to weaken. She didn't understand his effect on her but she knew it was dangerous. Far more dangerous than any risks she might be running in her plot to avenge herself on David.

"All I can say, sweetheart, is that it isn't my ego talking, it's that 'perception' you keep crediting me with," he half-smiled. "Won't you listen to it?"

"Rand, we aren't meant for each other. Not even for a night," Kalinda said sadly. "Can't you understand that? We're two entirely different people. You need an easy-going, outdoorsy sort of woman. Perhaps someone who is also an artist."

"And you're a high-powered, competitive female executive who likes the good things in life, right?" he finished for her with a knowing look. "A woman who knows what she wants in a relationship and doesn't think she's going to find it in me. After all, I'm a lazy, good-for-nothing, ski-bum-fisherman who sells a few artsy-craftsy things on the side to keep the wolf from the door. Completely lacking in the good old American work ethic."

Kalinda thought about the white Lotus and the expensively furnished home by the lake and refrained from inquiring as to the source of those things. She might not like the answer. The thought that she had met up with a professional gigolo and had almost let him make love to her was totally unnerving. She didn't want to know which rich lady tourist had paid for the Lotus last winter!

But even as she thought the worst of him, Kalinda knew she didn't have all the facts. She barely knew him. She would try to refrain from judging him. He had his own life to live just as she had hers.

"Rand, please, don't put words in my mouth. Let's just say we come from two different walks of life, okay? We should never have let ourselves get carried away like this on the basis of a simple physical attraction."

"Well, at least you're admitting we have got that much going for us!"

She smiled weakly, shaking her head in exasperation. "I can't very well deny that, can I? But it's not enough. I'm not in the market for a weekend affair and that's final. I think I'd better be getting back to the motel."

"What about dinner tonight?" he countered coolly. "I've already bought the steaks and the wine."

She looked at him helplessly. "And changed the sheets on the bed, too, I expect?"

He stared at her for a second and then grinned that engaging, slightly feral grin which was so unbelievably attractive on him. "How did you guess?"

"I have this strange feeling you've got the routine down pat!"

"No," he denied at once, sobering. "This time it's special. There's nothing routine about it. Please, Kalinda. Have dinner with me tonight."

"So you can spend the evening trying to talk me out of my plans?" she sighed.

"Yes."

"No thanks!"

"I swear I won't drag you off to bed." There was a meaningful pause. "Unless, of course, you decide that's where you belong, after all. Just promise to have dinner with me. I swear I won't muscle you into the bedroom."

"We'll only spend the time arguing over what I'm going to do tomorrow night," she protested, knowing she was weakening before the persuasiveness in him.

"Have you got anything better to do than argue with me?" he murmured, his fingers on her nape moving lightly, seductively. "Think of it as an opportunity to convince me you know what you're doing!"

"How can I refuse such a charming invitation!" she muttered dryly, wretchedly aware that spending the evening with him was exactly what she wanted to do, regardless of the complications involved.

"You high-powered female executives are all alike," he taunted on a soft rumble of laughter as he bent to brush his lips against hers. "Can't resist a challenge!"

Four

Rand was a man of his word, Kalinda decided much later that night as she grimly closed her motel room door and went to the window to watch the Lotus disappear into the night. Never had she spent an evening like the one he had just put her through!

She turned away from the window, letting the drape fall into place and morosely surveyed her room. It had been one line of reasoning after another, one argument after another, one persuasive attack on her logic after another. She felt utterly exhausted, she thought with a rueful grimace.

He had amazed her with his strategy, leaping nimbly from one point to the next in his efforts to convince her she was making a mistake in trying for revenge on David Hutton.

And, in spite of his hints to the contrary, Rand had not resorted again to seduction. Kalinda shook her head wryly. Instead, he had fed her well, spent several hours intently "discussing" the matter at hand, and then he'd left her on her doorstep with the most singly devastating comment of the evening.

"Ask yourself," he'd ordered softly as he'd opened her door for her, "why you're even bothering to listen to me in the first place. Face it, Kalinda, you want to be talked out of this fiasco. That's the reason you told me the truth this afternoon, isn't it? So that I could have a chance to play devil's advocate?"

He hadn't waited for her crushing retort. Instead, he'd vaulted easily down the steps, slid into the Lotus and disappeared. Leaving Kalinda behind to face a serious attack of self-honesty.

The depressing part about the evening, she thought as she slipped into the satin and lace nightgown and climbed into bed, was that all of his arguments were reasonable. It was a foolish and potentially dangerous scheme she had concocted. But even Rand hadn't hit on the one factor which was really troubling her about her own plans.

It was a factor which Kalinda had kept pushing into the background but which had become stronger than ever as Rand's arguments had weakened the rest of her logic. That factor was David Hutton's wife.

As Friday night approached, the unknown wife loomed larger and larger in Kalinda's mind. It was one of the reasons she'd arrived early at the rendezvous point. She'd wanted time to think about what she was doing. Time away from the pressures of work, from planning the party scheduled for the following week to entertain business associates, time away from her current and casual escorts of the moment.

She'd retreated to the mountains to convince herself she was doing the justifiable thing and here she'd met a man who probably should have been a prosecuting attorney instead of a part-time arts and crafts dealer!

Kalinda had never met Arleen Hutton but she knew a certain amount about her. At the time David had broken off the engagement there had been no lack of "friends" to tell Kalinda who'd taken her place.

Arleen was the daughter of a wealthy Colorado rancher. She'd brought money to the marriage, according the Kalinda's acquaintances, and she was reputed to be a very beautiful woman. She was also a few years younger than Kalinda.

It had been easy not to think about her, especially since Kalinda had no intention of actually trying to steal her husband away. But more and more frequently during the past week an insistent image had come to mind. The image of an innocent wife discovering her husband was meeting a woman at a remote mountain retreat.

Kalinda, blessed with an empathy she could have done well without in the business world, couldn't help wondering how she'd feel if she were that wife. And now Rand had systematically demolished all the reasons for revenge, leaving only the face of the unknown wife to haunt Kalinda's conscience.

Damn the man! She turned furiously over in bed, pounding the pillow with a disgusted fist. His talents truly had been wasted in life! With that sort of single-minded strength of purpose, he could have done just about anything he wanted in the world! But, she supposed thoughtfully, perhaps that's exactly what he *had* done. Perhaps he was quite content to fish and ski and make lovely pieces of pottery. And date rich tourists!

She lay staring at the ceiling for a long time after that, trying to recall the hurt and humiliation she'd felt two years ago. A hurt and humiliation that had come in the wake of the tragedy of her father's death and had, therefore, been all the more devastating. Kalinda's parents had been divorced several years previously and her mother had moved to Europe with her new husband the year Kalinda had gone off to college. Kalinda had faced both the tragedy and the humiliation quite alone.

But it was difficult tonight to resurrect those old feelings. The habit of wanting revenge was still there in her mind, but the emotions driving those feelings were gone. If she were completely honest with herself, Kalinda thought wonderingly, she'd realized they had been missing for some time. Two years of hard work and success had killed them rather effectively.

It had been only the habit that had made her jump at the opportunity of paying back David Hutton. Now, a combination of her conscience and the relentless arguments of a man she had only known for two days seemed to have succeeded in killing even the habit of wanting revenge. Kalinda thought once again of the unknown wife and of her own stupidity in wanting revenge on a man who wasn't worth the time of day. She made up her mind about what to do in the morning and went very soundly to sleep.

She dialed the private line number of David Hutton's office promptly at eight o'clock the next morning. He was there, just as she had expected him to be. Whatever else could be said of the man, he was a hard worker. It was one of the things she had admired about him in the beginning....

"David, this is Kalinda..." she began firmly, coolly.

"Getting impatient, darling?" he chuckled knowingly. "It won't be much longer now. I'm taking off around twelve. I'll be in the mountains by the middle of the afternoon. Enjoying yourself? Your office said you'd taken a couple of extra days.''

"I left that message in case you tried to get in touch with me," she affirmed. "But, David..."

"I can't wait to see you again, Kali. God, it's been a long time! I keep wondering what happened to us two years ago. We had so much going for us," he murmured deeply into the phone.

Kalinda gritted her teeth. He knew very well what had happened to them two years ago! He'd caused it to happen! But the momentary anger died quickly, leaving once again her newfound determination.

"David," she said calmly, "it's no good. I'm not going to meet you up here. I'm calling so you won't make the drive for nothing."

There was a fragment of stunned silence on the other end of the line and then David's voice came soothingly.

"This is hardly the time to get cold feet, Kali. We've got everything planned. Don't panic, darling. Just sit tight for a few more hours until I get there. We'll talk everything out. You'll see!"

Mentally Kalinda pictured him sitting behind his desk in the downtown highrise where his company had its headquarters. It was a handsome image in many respects. David Hutton was a good-looking man with dark brown hair and eyes. He would be thirty-six now and, unless he'd changed a lot in the past couple of years, still lean and dynamic. He dressed well, and admired those who did likewise. Two years ago Kalinda thought they would have made a good couple. It was with a small start that she realized this morning they would have made a disastrous couple. It would probably have been her David was planning to cheat today instead of the unknown woman who was his wife.

"I'm not getting cold feet, David. I've simply changed my mind." She'd decided earlier on the approach she would use. If she told David she'd only been plotting to make a fool of him, he would be infuriated and she didn't feel like putting up with that sort of scene. She would leave him with a sop for his ego, annoying as that course of action might be for her.

"Why, Kalinda?" he demanded with the first touch of a chill in his voice.

"It's wrong, David, and we both know it. There's your wife to consider, for one thing and there's the little matter of both our reputations. What if someone were to discover what's going on?"

"That's hardly likely," he growled forcefully. "And you don't have to concern yourself with my wife. I've never really talked to you about my marriage, darling. It's one of the things I wanted to discuss with you this weekend. It's...it's been something of a business arrangement,'' he hinted delicately as if casting out a lure.

Kalinda lifted one brow sardonically but said calmly into the phone, ''I'm afraid that's your problem, David. All I know is I don't want to be involved in a triangle....''

''Kali, honey, stop talking like that,'' he coaxed, sounding a little desperate and very determined. ''This is just between you and I. Now you stay put. I'll be up there in a few hours. I can get away earlier than planned. We'll talk this out in person.''

''Go ahead and drive up here, David, if you like. But I won't be here. I mean it, I'm not seeing you again.'' Kalinda felt her patience and reasonableness slipping away. The firmness in her words was unmistakable. ''Let's just agree we were on the verge of doing something we both would have regretted and let it go at that.''

''No! Kali, listen to me. You would never have agreed to see me again if you weren't still interested. You know that. We can recapture what we once had if we only give it a chance...''

''Oh, go to hell, David!'' she finally snapped, disgusted with him and with herself for having gotten into the mess. ''Do you want to know the real reason I agreed to meet you up here? I was going to let you drive all the way up with notions of starting an affair and then I was going to encourage you to think I was equally interested. I was going to let you wine and dine me, make you think you were on the point of seducing me and then I was going to laugh in your face! I never had any intention of rekindling our old romance, you idiot! How could I after what you did two years ago? You destroyed whatever we might have had together and I have no interest in raking through the ashes. Good-bye, David. Don't call me again!''

She set the receiver firmly back into the cradle and surged irritably to her feet. Dammit! She hadn't meant to wind up the phone call that way, but he'd asked for it. She wanted out of the awkward situation and she'd offered him a reasonable way of calling it quits. He had only himself to blame for having annoyed her to the point where she'd told him the truth.

She glanced around the small hotel room, impatient to escape now that the decision had been made and action taken. She wanted away from these mountains, away from the scene of the canceled fiasco.

She went to the closet and began packing the chocolate leather luggage. She wore the white cotton tuxedo shirt she'd had on the first day with the khaki trousers and her hair was in the neat twist behind one ear. She felt as cool and self-confident as she looked. She had made the right decision.

Or had it made for her, she reflected ruefully,

thinking of Rand Alastair as she swung the soft leather case into her silver Mercedes.

By the time she checked out of the motel it was nearly nine o'clock. She climbed behind the wheel of the car and wondered what Rand was doing. Was he thinking about her? Concerned about what her final decision would be?

Kalinda sat quietly in the seat before starting the engine, staring straight ahead through the windshield and thinking about Rand. She would never see him again and that seemed rather strange, considering the effect he'd had on her during the past two days.

But it was for the best, of course. There was no chance for anything solid and lasting between them. He was obviously content to live the undemanding life here in the mountains and she was born to thrive in the city. There would be other lady tourists to amuse him and with the coming of ski season he'd probably have to close up the shop completely in order to handle both his skiing and his dates, she told herself grimly.

With a decisive gesture she started the engine and backed the car out of its slot. No, Rand wasn't her sort of man by a long shot. She needed someone altogether more like herself. And she didn't need an affair that came to life only on the weekends she managed to drive up into the mountains.

But somehow Kalinda wasn't altogether surprised to find herself guiding the silver car along the narrow lakeside road toward Rand's home. She would only stop long enough to say good-bye, she told herself. He deserved to know his arguments had been effective. She really believed he'd been genuinely concerned for her in this matter.

She was still justifying her reasons for stopping to say farewell several minutes later as she parked the Mercedes next to the Lotus and opened the door. The sight of the sleek, white sports car brought up the depressing image of a professional gigolo again and Kalinda told herself she was absolutely right in her decision not to see Rand again after this morning. Two ships passing in the night.

The morning sunlight was coming cheerfully through the swaying pines as she knocked tentatively on the door. She really didn't know that much about his habits, Kalinda thought as she waited for a response. Perhaps he'd gone fishing. Or perhaps he was still asleep. Maybe today he would rouse himself sufficiently to open the gallery.

She was running through the list of possibilities for not finding him at home when the door was abruptly flung open.

Whatever Kalinda had planned to say was squelched before she could form the words by the sight of him standing on the threshold staring at her. He looked terrible! The chestnut hair was ruffled as if he'd been combing his hand through it. The hazel eyes were dark and strained and there was a desperately tired, haggard look about him which caught at her heart. He was wearing the faded jeans and an unbuttoned white shirt with the sleeves rolled up. He held a cup of coffee in one hand.

In the instant of silent regard that passed between them, Kalinda felt the taut emotion vibrating in the atmosphere. She met his eyes and began a frantic search for something reasonable to say. He didn't look at all reasonable, however.

"Rand, I...I only stopped to tell..." she began.

His hand fell away from the door and the cup of coffee was set down on a nearby stand. The hazel eyes flared to life with a deep, hungry gleam as he reached for her.

"You came to tell me you've changed your mind about meeting Hutton tonight at the motel," he stated evenly, his fingers sliding around her neck while his thumbs went under her jaw to hold her face so that she could not look away.

"Yes," she said simply, feeling the currents of physical awareness passing through her. He looked awful, she told herself again, and somehow he made her want to take him in her arms and comfort him. How could that be?

"It's about time you got here," he whispered thickly, pulling her gently, inexorably toward him. "I've spent most of the night walking the floor over you, Kalinda Brady. Thank God you've finally decided to put me out of my misery!''

His mouth came heavily down on hers before she could think of a way to respond to his words. And as soon as she felt his warm, aggressive passion flood her senses, Kalinda realized this was the real reason she'd talked herself into saying good-bye to him.

"I was sure I could get you to make the right decision," he said huskily against her lips. "So sure. But there was always the possibility I'd guessed wrong."

"Are you often wrong about people?" she asked softly, her hands sliding up his chest, pushing aside the loosely hanging shirt.

"Very seldom," he replied equally softly. "But it's never been quite this important to be right before!"

Then his mouth closed fiercely over hers once more, the tip of his probing tongue flicking across her lips and ultimately claiming the inner warmth of her mouth.

Kalinda shivered beneath the onslaught, thrusting aside her common sense and knowing as she felt his hands move on her that this morning she was going to surrender to the pull of an intense passion she'd never known before.

He heard the soft sigh with which she accepted the reality of their desire and Rand folded her tightly, tenderly against him, an answering groan of need deep in his chest.

His fingers found the line of her spine and tracked upward, sending out little eddies of sensuous current at every point along the way. Kalinda felt him arch her against his lower body and she moaned her aching response.

"I've wanted you from the moment I saw you," he breathed, stringing slow, damp little kisses along her cheek to the nape of her neck. With one strong hand he held her face buried in his shoulder while his teeth nipped erotically at the vulnerable neck he was baring.

The tuxedo-styled shirt and lacy bra seemed to float free of her body, leaving her nude from the waist up. The morning sunlight danced along the silky skin of her shoulders and she heard Rand's indrawn breath. Gently he freed her hair.

"I'm exhausted from pacing my floor; I've had so much coffee it's a wonder I'm able to think at all. Never in my life have I had so many doubts about my own judgment, but suddenly I feel fantastic," Rand growled as she played her fingers across the muscles of his back, her hands moving under the white shirt.

"Oh, Rand," she breathed helplessly, finding his tanned throat with her questing lips. "I shouldn't be here…"

"But you are and that's all that counts," he interrupted in a passion-roughened voice. He trembled beneath the touch of her lips and Kalinda was thrilled to be able to arouse him as he aroused her. It was crazy and it could only happen between them once but she was twenty-nine years old and she was suddenly determined to sample the depths of true desire. All the arguments against one-time encounters with virtual strangers could be dragged out later when she was back in the reality of Denver. This was a stolen moment out of time that would never come her way again. How could she pass it by?

"Kalinda, Kalinda, I want you so much and I was so afraid at times during the night that you wouldn't come to me...."

She shook her head wordlessly, her lashes dusting her cheeks as she lowered her eyes from the flaming want in his gaze. She hadn't known herself that she would come to him like this. Nor did she want to think about her own actions in that moment. Instead she clung to him with an intensity that amazed her. She felt the lean strength in his hips as her hands searched out the feel of him beneath the tight jeans.

"Why are we standing here? I have the perfect place for us," he rasped and swung her high into his arms. Kalinda pressed her lips to his now-naked shoulder and closed her eyes once more as he strode down the cream-carpeted hall to a bedroom full of caramels and browns.

He settled her gently on the sun-dappled bed, her light-colored hair fanning out across the rich golden brown bedspread. For a moment he stood gazing down at her and then he sat beside her, his hands going to the long tendrils of hair.

"It's almost the same color as my bedspread," he half-smiled, stroking luxuriously. "Your skin looks like cream in the morning light." His eyes roamed warmly over her as he slowly unbuckled the web belt of her khaki trousers and finished undressing her.

He performed the task with infinite care, pausing to caress each inch of skin revealed until she lay naked beneath his hands. He stroked his fingers in languid, delicious little circles along the length of her leg from ankle to thigh. By the time he reached her hip Kalinda was trembling with desire.

Apparently satisfied with his efforts, Rand pulled away for a moment, sliding quickly, impatiently out of his jeans and returning to her welcoming arms with a hoarsely whispered exclamation of need.

"I was going to head straight back to Denver after calling David this morning," she whispered as he gathered her close. "But somehow I couldn't leave without seeing you...."

"I would have gone mad if you hadn't."

He buried his lips at the curve of her shoulder, nipping gently at her skin while his hand closed possessively over her breast. The firming nipple beneath his palm seemed to arouse him further and Kalinda reached down to touch him with intimate wonder.

"Did you really spend the night pacing the floor?" she asked breathlessly, as his body stirred ardently against hers.

"What does it look like?" he growled ruefully. "But it was worth it to open the door this morning and find you standing there. I took one look at you and knew I didn't have to worry any longer!"

He raked a trail of pleasure across the taut nipple, down her sensitive stomach and along her thigh, following his hand with his lips. Her fingers twisted passionately in his hair as he slid lower on her body and when his exciting kisses found her secret core of desire she cried out.

"Oh, my God, Rand! You're driving me wild. I've never known this kind of...of *aching!*"

He turned his head and kissed the inside of her thigh. Her leg shifted reflexively, her knee lifting alongside his body.

"I know exactly what you're talking about," he murmured thickly, his fingers squeezing into the softness of her curving bottom. "After I took you back to the motel last night I told myself I was a fool, that I should have kept you here and taken you to bed regardless of what you thought you wanted at the time. But I knew it would be better if it happened this way...."

"You seem to have known me better than I knew myself for a while," she admitted, twisting restlessly against him. Her breathing came in short, broken little pants as she felt the raging hunger take control of her.

"And now I'm going to know you even more thoroughly," he vowed. "I'm going to make you mine this morning, Kalinda Brady. I have to!"

She saw the smoldering fire in his eyes as he raised himself with sudden intention and her own whirling senses spun chaotically out of control.

Rand trapped her ankle with his leg and an instant later he settled along the length of her, covering her soft, curving body with his hard, thrilling strength.

But even as she reached up to cling to him and draw him down to her, Kalinda was aware that he was determined to hold off the ultimate union a little longer.

"Please," she whimpered, becoming incredibly aroused as he stoked the fire in her even higher. "Please, Rand I...I *need* you!"

His response was to move against her with a teasing, provoking movement that nearly drove her out of her mind when he failed to complete it.

"Tell me," he commanded, a yearning tone lacing the fierce order. "Tell me how much you need me, how much you want me...."

"More than I've ever wanted any man," she

confessed raggedly, her head thrown back against the pillow, her body arching with consummate pleading into his. "I've never even known how... how *necessary* it could be!" That was nothing less than the shattering truth. Never had she felt like this, wanted a man so desperately.

"That's how I need you," he swore deeply. "I had to hear you say it. I had to *know!*"

His hands gripped her shoulders and his body surged passionately against hers, claiming it utterly and completely. Kalinda's breath caught in her throat and she could only cling and cling and cling to the powerful masculine body. Instinctively she sought to envelope his strength, make him a part of her.

Rand held her so tightly they seemed to merge into one being. He licked at the sheen of perspiration that shimmered on the slope of her breast as he set the rhythm of their desire.

"My God, sweetheart," he groaned. "You're flaming like a torch for me!"

Kalinda could only gasp her wonder and desire. No man had ever beckoned to her deepest needs with the irresistible lure of such honest and overwhelming male hunger. It was primitive and it was real yet it was astonishingly tender at times. It cut through all the layers of civilization and sophistication.

She cried out as the threshold was reached, her

body shivering with a sudden convulsive energy she'd never known before. It arched her throat, tautened every muscle in her and brought a mind-spinning sense of release.

Above her she heard the harsh, muffled shout of satisfaction and male triumph as Rand followed her over the magic threshold, wrapping her tightly to him in preparation for the long, languid descent on the other side.

"Kalinda, my sweet Kalinda," he breathed over and over again as the sunlight played across their damp, naked bodies. The fragrance of the mountains drifted through the open window, combining with the earthy, honest scent of their passion and Kalinda inhaled it deeply.

"Tell me the truth," Rand grated urgently. "Do you have any regrets about not seeing that other man? Any at all?"

She turned against him, lifting her eyes to meet the surprisingly vulnerable expression in his own.

"None," she smiled softly.

He closed his coppery lashes for a long moment and she felt the gratitude in him.

"You had me so damn scared," he admitted wryly, leaning back against the pillows to stare intently at the ceiling. "So damn scared!"

"Somehow I can't envision you scared of anything," she retorted lightly.

"You should have seen me at four this morning!"

"Were you really so concerned about me?"

"If you hadn't shown up here or at the shop by this afternoon, I would have taken matters in my own hands. I couldn't let you meet him, Kalinda. It would have been so dangerous!" He shook his head once on the pillow as if awed by the near miss.

"I appreciate your interest," she murmured gently, "but it really wasn't that big a risk! He's simply not the violent sort!"

"You're a little naive, sweetheart, but that's okay," he half-grinned, lifting a hand to ruffle her already tangled hair as he turned to look at her. "Even if you were right about his degree of potential violence, there was my other, equally strong fear!"

"That I'd fall back under his spell? That was never a possibility, Rand. Believe me."

"But you still felt so strongly about him," he persisted.

"No, talking to you made me realize all I felt was the *habit* of hating him. The feeling that he ought to be punished. But it was a hollow sort of emotion. It was a relief to call the whole thing off. Then, too, I kept thinking about his poor wife. In the end, I just thanked my lucky stars I wasn't in her shoes as I so easily could have been."

"How did he take it when you phoned him this morning?"

Kalinda lifted one bare shoulder dismissingly. "He wasn't very pleased. I gave him all the logical reasons why we shouldn't meet. His wife, our reputations. I tried to make it sound as if two reasonable people should agree to call the whole thing off before it got started."

"Did he buy it?" There was a wary look in the hazel eyes as they narrowed slightly.

"He kept trying to talk me into staying here until he could arrive and talk me around," she confessed. "I finally got fed up and told him the truth, that I had agreed to the weekend in the first place because I wanted a little revenge for the way he'd treated me two years ago. Then I told him not to call me again and hung up the phone."

"Hmmm."

"What's that supposed to mean?" she demanded, mouth curving at his skeptical tone.

"Forget it, honey. We'll talk about it later." He yawned extravagantly. "Hell, I'm exhausted! You wore me out," he chuckled affectionately.

"You wore yourself out pacing a floor for no reason at all!"

"Oh, I had my reasons," he retorted sleepily. "But my reasons are all tucked safely into my bed for the moment. Will you think I'm a callous brute if I grab a nap, honey?" He slanted her a pleading glance.

He looked so sleepy that Kalinda found herself smiling with a tenderness she'd never felt toward a man. Almost lovingly she stroked the angled plane of his cheek.

"No."

"We've got a lot to discuss," he murmured, already half-asleep.

Kalinda felt the moisture behind her lashes and blinked it away determinedly. She waited until she felt his hold on her loosen and knew for certain he was making up for the sleep he'd missed the previous night.

Then, aware there could be only one ending for this kind of passionate interlude, she slowly rose from the caramel bedspread and began to dress.

Five

Kalinda stood at the window of her office in downtown Denver and looked out across the Mile-High City with remote eyes. Situated on the plains with the mountains nearby to the west, Denver had become the lively, thriving headquarters of the business empire of the Rocky Mountain states.

The swirl of new money from the energy boom which had so affected the city had, in turn, stimulated other businesses. Gleaming highrise buildings in the downtown area gave evidence of the investment capital pouring into the area.

Oil, coal and uranium had beckoned the modern prospectors and speculators. In the last century it had been the lure of gold. But Denver's residents, while they may have been lured to the gateway city by the promise of new opportunities, soon became a fiercely loyal lot for other reasons.

Not the least of those reasons was the city's proximity to the fabulous vacation areas of the Rockies. During the winter the mountains offered some of the finest powder snow for skiing that could be found in the world. Many claimed the Colorado mountains were the United States' equivalent of Europe's Alps. During the summer those same mountains were a breathtaking wonderland of craggy peaks and green valleys.

And that, Kalinda thought with disgust as she turned away from the window, was all she seemed to be able to think about for the past two days. The mountains. Was she doomed to remember the man she had met there everytime she looked out her window?

How long did it take to recover from a weekend fling? she asked herself for the thousandth time as she poured a cup of tea and moodily surveyed her office. It was an attractive office with gold carpet and a heavy mahogany desk she had inherited when she took over her father's role. The colors weren't hers, but there had been more important uses for the company's funds during the past two years than redecorating the president's quarters!

She sipped her tea, staring at the report in front of her and told herself she was going to have to put

Rand Alastair out of her head once and for all. And
the most efficient way of doing that was by throwing herself back into her work. She should be worrying about the cocktail party she was giving that
evening, not dwelling on the exhausted features of
the man she had left sleeping in the house by the
lake. Determinedly Kalinda brought her well-
developed powers of concentration to bear on the
company's recent audit report. She wanted the
numbers clear in her head when she met with the
members of the board later that week.

She was well into the matter at hand when the
intercom chimed softly on her desk.

"Yes, George?" she said absently into the
speaker, her eyes still on the figures in front of her.

"There's a call from Mr. David Hutton, Miss
Brady. Will you take it?" George Barrett's calm,
efficient manner was laced with just a hint of his
own feelings on the subject. George, to the astonishment of almost everyone, had turned out to be
the perfect secretary. He saw himself as breaking
the sexual discrimination barriers in reverse and
strove tirelessly for professionalism and compe-
tency. He never allowed a hint of his personal
thoughts to interfere in the conduct of business unless he sensed something crucial was at stake.

Over the past few months, ever since Kalinda had
hired him for the permanent position after he'd been
sent as a temporary by an agency, Kalinda had

come to respect George's instincts. He knew she was routinely refusing calls from David Hutton. He must have a reason for bothering to check with her now to see if she had suddenly changed her mind.

"What's wrong, George?" she asked quietly, switching her attention completely to the little intercom. "You know I have no wish to accept his calls."

George hesitated. She could visualize him in the outer office wearing his three-piece suit and dominating the entrance to the inner sanctum. He was a young man, about twenty-five, pleasant looking and serenely competent. The other office workers had eyed him skeptically from the start but he was now a well-accepted figure in their day-to-day world. In fact, Kalinda knew, he had recently had to set down some very strict rules. Not for Kalinda's sake, but for his own. George had become quite popular with the women on the staff.

"I don't believe this call is of a personal nature, Miss Brady," he finally announced formally. "He won't explain the reason but there's something else involved. I can tell."

Kalinda gritted her teeth and then sighed in resignation. "Okay, put him through. If you're wrong about this, George..."

"I know," George interrupted, unbending slightly at the mild threat in her words. "I'll be the one who has to explain why you hung up on him."

Kalinda grinned and took the call.

"What is it, David?" she asked without preamble, her voice turning cold and crisp.

"It's about time you took my call," he drawled. "That damn secretary of yours has been putting me off for two days!"

"On my instructions. Now that you're through, will you please state your business and get off the line? We really don't have anything to say to each other." Kalinda realized vaguely that her only feeling toward David Hutton now was one of impatience. The thirst for revenge that had driven her into the mountains last weekend had been well and truly eradicated. Another reason why it would be difficult to stop thinking about Rand Alastair.

"Business is exactly why I'm calling, darling," he murmured, and something in his tone chilled her. "You should have met me at that motel, Kalinda. Things could have been handled a lot more pleasantly if you had."

"What in the world are you talking about?"

"A merger, Kalinda. You've done some astonishing things with Brady Data Processing. Two years ago everyone said it had no choice but to go under. You've created a total turnaround situation and your company, my love, has become one very enticing little pigeon. I want it."

Kalinda swallowed in shock and outrage. It was several seconds before she could control her anger into an icy refusal. "Out of the question. Brady Data Processing is not interested in merging with anyone, David, and quite definitely not your firm!"

"You aren't going to have any choice. I'm filing forms with the Securities and Exchange Commission this week."

"What!" Kalinda stared at the phone. Filing forms with the SEC? There could be only one reason for that...

"That's right, love," he taunted with pleased satisfaction. "I'm going to force the merger on you since you weren't willing to discuss it under more amicable conditions."

"You mean since I wasn't willing to give you an opportunity of trying to seduce me into surrendering the company without a fight!"

"Precisely," he agreed smoothly. "I would have preferred a 'friendly' sort of takeover but since you've proven obstinate, you may as well know I don't mind a fight. It will cost more this way, of course, because I shall have to offer a premium price for your stock, but it will be worth it in the end."

"How much of the outstanding stock have you picked up already?" Kalinda forced herself to ask bravely.

"Just under the five percent limit," he acknowledged easily.

She winced. Anyone going after more than five

percent of a publicly held stock had to register that intention with the SEC. Hence the papers David claimed to be filing. He could now start hunting down vast quantities of the shares on the open market. All he needed were enough to give him control of the firm. Kalinda felt the panic begin to rise in her. After all her work in getting Brady Data Processing back on its feet! She couldn't bear the thought of having it forcibly taken from her. What about all the people who worked for her? Company morale would go to hell when word of this leaked out. Nothing sent shivers of fear through a firm faster than rumors of an intended hostile takeover move. And there were so few defenses for a company in Brady's position.

"Why are you doing this, David?" she asked coldly, trying desperately to think of defense tactics. She knew so little of this sort of thing. She'd never faced it before.

"The usual reasons," he retorted bluntly. "My firm is heavy in cash right now and we need some acquisitions. I've seen your balance sheet, darling, and you are ripe."

"You're telling me there's nothing personal in this, right? Just business?" she scoffed angrily.

"Oh, no, I wouldn't say that," he chuckled arrogantly. "It will give me great personal satisfaction to take Brady Data Processing. It should have been mine two years ago."

"You didn't want it two years ago!" she flung back.

"I've changed my mind. Thanks to you, Kalinda. No one thought you could pull it off, you know. Everyone was sure that firm was headed for the bottom. But now that you've done all the hard work…"

"You think you can just step in and help yourself? I've got news for you, David. We'll fight."

"They all say that in the beginning. Go ahead, love. It will only make the process that much more interesting. Perhaps somewhere along the line you'll even consider that little mountain rendezvous we planned. Now *that* would be amusing, wouldn't it? I wonder how many chief executive officers of firms facing a hostile merger have tried to buy off the raiding company with their bodies? Interesting thought, isn't it…?"

Kalinda slammed the phone down, his confident, knowing laughter ringing in her ears.

She sat in stunned silence for several minutes, gazing with unseeing eyes at the framed mirror on the opposite wall. It reflected her well-tailored white business suit with its narrow skirt and close-fitting jacket. Her hair was up, as usual, and the yellow silk blouse she wore was open at the neck with a rakish air.

My God, she thought dazedly. What did she do now? Handling hostile mergers wasn't one of those subjects stressed when she had been in business management school. It was something one learned on the streets, a true urban guerrilla warfare. She knew all about building a company up from within, obtaining capital, promoting research, making the firm's stock appear attractive to the analysts of brokerage houses so that they would, in turn, encourage investors to buy it; she knew about those things. She'd learned some the hard way and some she'd studied in school.

But this was a different kind of game. Unfriendly mergers were something that happened to other companies, not to one's own! She closed her eyes briefly in self-reprisal. She had made a bad error in not planning ahead for such an eventuality. But she had been so swamped just trying to save the business it had never occurred to her that someone would come along and take the salvage prize right out of her hands.

Not to mention the hands of the loyal management. Breaking the news to them would be the hardest part. It was their jobs, after all, which were most likely to be destroyed by such an action. The rank and file were probably the safest. They would be needed to keep things running. But all those in management positions who had worked their way up during the years would find themselves in real jeopardy. They could be replaced and most likely would be by aggressive young movers from the acquiring firm.

Everything she had worked for during the past two years would be gone. Kalinda, of course, would be the first to go...

But that was negative thinking, she told herself furiously, getting restlessly to her feet and walking back to the window. She was going to fight. She had to. She owed it to her company to try to save its independence. Tomorrow morning she would call in the company officers for an emergency strategy meeting. She shook her head sadly. It was going to be a shock for all of them.

But in spite of the crisis and the need for planning, there was nothing she could realistically do that evening. She couldn't very well call off the party and it wouldn't do her any good even if she could. Grimly she paced back to her desk.

Several hours later Kalinda paused in her duties as hostess to take stock of the cocktail party's success. There were several important business associates here this evening, many of them male and that meant she had to be especially nice to their wives. The last thing she wanted was to risk a case of wifely jealousy. She had walked a fine line for two years and thought she'd done a good job of reassuring suspicious wives and still maintaining the solid business contacts she needed.

She glanced around the room, taking in the well-dressed, affluent crowd in their expensive suits and gowns, wondering who among them she might go to for advice and professional consultation. She needed to talk to someone, she thought. Someone who knew about the dirty in-fighting that went on in a hostile merger situation. It was a cinch she wouldn't get much constructive help from her own staff. They'd never encountered such a maneuver.

Before she could decide if there was someone in the crowd who could be potentially helpful, Kalinda was interrupted by the effusive thanks of a charming, older woman who glided up to her in a cloud of perfume and wispy chiffon.

"Kalinda, my dear! Thank you so much for the lovely picture you gave Harold and I! So nice of you to think of us while you were on vacation! But your dear father was like that, too. Always so thoughtful of others."

"I'm glad you like it," Kalinda smiled, thinking of the price she'd paid for the watercolor she'd purchased in Rand's gallery. A weekend affair...

"It looks perfect in Harold's den! And you look quite perfect yourself tonight," Mrs. Sebastian added with a warm smile, surveying her hostess's printed beet-red silk jacquard sheath with its touches of peacock blue. A fine gold braid edged the neckline and wrists. It was a sumptuous, almost oriental effect which Kalinda wore well. The buttery material slid fluidly over her small breasts and rounded hips.

"Thank you," Kalinda said, hastening to return the compliment. She stood talking for several minutes to the wife of one of her top managers and then edged away with the excuse of checking the buffet table.

Around her the crowd swirled happily amid the lush green and ripe apricot décor of the town house. The green in the plush rug gave the apricot print-covered furniture a dramatic background. The color scheme emphasized the focal point of the room which was a huge sun parlor that formed one entire wall.

Brilliant patches of white had been used sparingly against the rich colors in the form of an occasional lamp and glass-topped coffee table. The dining table was also a stark white and stood in front of a mirrored wall which reflected the colorful buffet food set out on it.

As usual, Kalinda spared no expense when she entertained, deeming it a business necessity. But even she had to smile at that justification. The truth was, she enjoyed entertaining. Tonight was an exception. But, then, who could take pleasure in such things with a sword hanging over one's head?

Only a few people knew that she, herself, prepared the elegant little canapés and hors d'oeuvres served at her parties. Others just seemed to assume she used a caterer and she let them think that. Only she knew that such gourmet cooking was a source of relaxation for her. She had discovered it during the past year and was continually amazed at how she could escape her business concerns for a few hours in a kitchen.

Across the room she caught Colin Wayne's eye and smiled at him as he advanced. She had gone out with him on a couple of occasions recently and found his easy charm made for pleasant evenings. He was in his early thirties, with carefully styled blond hair and laughing blue eyes. He was also, she had discovered, a brilliant player on the lively Denver Stock Exchange.

"Another great party, Kalinda," he grinned approvingly, reaching behind her to help himself to a little cracker covered with rich, dark caviar. "Beats me how you throw these affairs together so easily when you work so hard! You'd have made a great corporate wife, you know!"

"You've got a lot of nerve eating my food and insulting me at the same time!" she grumbled in response to his teasing.

"I know, I know, you'd rather be a great corporate manager than a great corporate wife. But that's only because you haven't met the right man. Someday..."

"Have some more caviar," she advised dryly.

"We both know I'd be bored to tears as a house-wife!"

"How can I argue with that? I'd feel the same," he laughed.

"It is rather difficult to picture you as a house-wife," she agreed.

"Still," he went on jokingly, "if I can find my-self a woman who can keep me in the style to which I would like to become accustomed…" He glanced meaningfully around the elegant town house and back at Kalinda who narrowed her eyes at him in mock warning.

"Don't look at me," she said hastily.

"How about a business marriage?" he suggested brightly, munching more caviar. "I can keep track of your company's stock movements for you and you can do things that make it move. Preferably upward. Which it seemed to be doing this past week," he added slyly.

She glanced at him quickly and then deliberately forced a smile. "You noticed."

"That volume was picking up? Yes. And the price went up a bit, too. Something I should know, love? Always happy to help spread the good word if it will raise a stock's price. Got something new coming out on the market?"

"It's nice to know you love me for myself and not for business reasons," she mocked, hiding a wince as she realized the activity in her company's stock was undoubtedly from David's move to start buying shares.

"No reason the two can't be combined," he observed cheerfully.

"Well, I hate to disappoint you, but there's no smashing new product about to hit the market. I guess the stock activity is just a matter of people knowing a good investment when they see it," she tried to say lightly. She didn't want to discuss the merger with Colin or anyone else until she knew what she was going to do, how she was going to react. Dammit! She needed professional advice. There were law firms and investment bankers who specialized in this sort of thing. If she just knew someone who could point her in the right direction! The sense of panic had to be forcefully fought back down.

"No hot tips, huh?" he asked sadly.

"Not tonight," she retorted firmly, wondering why she had hardly even given Colin a passing thought since she'd returned from the mountains. But she knew the answer to that, she told herself honestly. It was going to be a long time before she thought of him in a romantic context again. How long was the image of Rand Alastair going to dominate her? She supposed that, even with a full-fledged business crisis facing her, he would be the last thing she thought of before she went to sleep tonight. Just as he had been last night and the night before that.

"Well, how about a hot date, instead?" Colin countered with a laughing leer. "That new French place sounds interesting."

Kalinda's mouth curved ruefully. "Can I let you know, Colin? I'm going to be very busy this week and I really don't know my schedule yet." It was the only way she could think of to phrase the excuse.

His good-looking features contrived to appear disappointed and philosophical at the same time. "Ah, well. Perhaps next week?"

"I'll check my calendar," she promised apologetically.

"The perils of dating a lady executive," he groaned and glanced automatically toward the door as a knock sounded. "Looks like you've got a late arrival."

Kalinda frowned, unable to think of anyone still unaccounted for. "Excuse me. I'll see who it is."

She crossed the lush green carpet, skirting a chatting cluster of guests and reached for the doorknob, an automatic smile on her face as she opened it.

The polite words of welcome died in her throat as the light spilled over the figure in her doorway. Chestnut hair gleamed from a recent shower, chestnut hair that had been trimmed and carefully combed since she'd seen it last. The light-colored suit looked hand-tailored and was complimented by a satin bow tie. The crisp white shirt was understated and elegant.

"Rand," she whispered finally. "What are you doing here?"

"That's obvious, isn't it?" he murmured, hazel eyes regarding her with an intent, considering expression. "I'm here to rescue you."

"Rescue me!" she squeaked, still trying to recover from the initial shock of seeing him on her doorstep. She stared up at him, dumbfounded, unable to comprehend his meaning. Why had he come like this? It was going to be hard enough getting over him without seeing him again. But if he tried to prolong the hopeless affair it would be impossible.

He lifted his hand and she saw for the first time he was carrying an orchid; one very perfect, very exotic, very brilliant golden orchid. He smiled as she instinctively put out her hand to accept the proffered gift.

"Honey," he murmured softly, putting both hands lightly on her shoulders and pulling her close long enough to drop a warm, hungry kiss on her astonished, parted lips, "if you don't even know yet that you need rescuing, you're in worse trouble than I thought!"

"Oh, Rand, you shouldn't have come," she heard herself whisper brokenly. "This is crazy. It's going to make everything so much harder..." She lifted misty-gray eyes to his.

"Hadn't you better let me in?" he drawled invitingly. "Your guests are beginning to wonder if I'm a traveling salesman you're trying to get rid of!"

Unwillingly, Kalinda smiled. "I don't get many salesmen dressed like that!" That much was the truth, she thought vaguely. Rand could hold his own with anyone else in the room tonight. She wondered why he had invested in such a wardrobe for the mountains. But, then, it rather went with the Lotus. She shook her head in confusion.

"I don't know what you're doing here," she began firmly, feeling a new kind of panic. "But it's all wrong. Can't you see? You shouldn't have come after me. I won't...I won't have an affair with you, Rand. We're totally unsuited. I should never have gone to your house that morning..." she broke off helplessly under the impact of the memory that flamed warmly in his eyes.

"Personally, I happen to think that was the only smart thing you did last weekend! Now move out of the doorway, sweetheart, and let your rescuer inside."

Unable to think of anything else to do, Kalinda did as instructed.

"Got anything to eat?" Rand went on easily, taking in the crowded room with a single, sweeping glance. "I'm starved."

"Over there," she admitted, gesturing toward the long white table in front of the mirrored wall. "Help yourself," she added wryly. She still held the golden orchid clutched in her hand.

He put a proprietary hand on her lower back and urged her forward. "Stop looking like a cornered kitten. I'm friendly, remember? Although why I should be after waking up and finding you'd run off…"

"I'd rather we didn't discuss that," she began stiffly.

"You want to discuss the rescue operation instead?" he invited, bringing her to a halt beside the buffet and perusing it with keen interest.

"What are you talking about? What rescue?" she finally managed a little blankly. He was throwing one curve after another tonight.

"The rescue of Brady Data Processing from the grasping talons of a corporate raider, naturally." Rand reached for a salmon and cucumber canapé. Several of them.

Kalinda stared at him, openmouthed. "How in the world did you know about that?" she breathed.

"There had to be a reason Hutton wanted to try his hand at seducing you after all this time. When you told me a little about the history of your firm and Hutton's newly aroused interest in you, I got suspicious. I asked you to consider the fact that it might be the business he was after, if you'll recall.''

"Well, yes, I know, but I never dreamed…'' Kalinda sighed. "You have no idea how shocked I was when he called today!''

"Sure I do,'' he contradicted calmly, slanting a glance at her. "It always hits the unsuspecting ones like a ton of bricks.''

"But how did you know what was going on?''

"Monday I did some checking. There's always someone in a company who will talk. I got hold of one of Hutton's vice-presidents.''

"Just like that?'' she demanded.

"Just like that.''

"You'll excuse me if I seem to be having a hard time taking all this in!'' she snapped, growing a little irritated over his complacency. The shock of finding him on her doorstep was wearing off to be replaced by confusion. She thought she understood this man. How was it he was surprising her like this? What did he know of the high-powered business world?

"Take your time.'' He reached for another morsel from the table.

"Thanks!'' she muttered and then took a short rein on her temper in favor of an attempt at reason. "Rand, what do you know about all this? What do you mean by 'rescuing me'?''

"If there's anything that can be done, I'll do it," he promised simply, munching contentedly.

"But how is it you know what to do?" she almost wailed.

He stopped munching for a moment and eyed her thoughtfully. Then he swallowed politely and a slow smile shaped his mouth.

"All it takes is total ruthlessness, an instinct for making war, and a willingness to stop at nothing."

Kalinda's eyes widened as she momentarily sensed a menace in him she hadn't dreamed existed. An instant later she shook her head, telling herself she was mistaken.

"But you don't have any of those awful qualifications, Rand," she smiled wanly, thinking of his leisurely, undemanding lifestyle. If he'd had any of those qualities he would have been making his living in a far different manner than the one he'd chosen.

"Want to bet? Watch this."

Something flickered in the hazel eyes, hardening, turning unbelievably cold. The smile he wore became far more dangerous than Kalinda would have believed possible. "What would Brady management think if the members discovered that their president had arranged to spend the weekend at a secluded motel with the head of the firm which is trying to force a merger? They might be forgiven for believing they'd been sold down the river, don't you agree? I'd say there's a good chance they might turn on their little lady chief executive officer, lose all confidence in her, and make it utterly impossible for her to rally the firm for the coming battle. The company would fall into Hutton's lap with only a whimper.''

"Rand!" Kalinda couldn't believe what she was hearing. No! The problem was she *could* believe it. There was something in him that proclaimed him capable of such an action and the knowledge shook her deeply. "You...you wouldn't do anything like that..."

"I might," he countered lazily. "If you don't agree to continue the affair we started last weekend!"

Six

The chattering, happy crowd seemed to recede into the distance as Kalinda forgot about everyone else in the room and stared, appalled at her uninvited guest.

"Are you saying you'd blackmail me into an affair?" she finally whispered.

He continued to regard her with that incredibly ruthless expression, everything about him hard, unyielding, and determined. Rand said nothing. He didn't need to say anything. The message was plain.

Shakily Kalinda reached out to steady herself with a hand on the edge of the white table. "I...I would never have thought you capable of doing anything like this."

"Perhaps in the short time we spent together you didn't get a chance to know me as well as you might have," he suggested coolly.

"No," she got out, her words barely a thread of sound as she tried to think what to do, how to handle him. "No, perhaps I didn't."

"Now you're seeing another side of me. Do you believe this side is capable of a certain ruthlessness?" he persisted.

"Yes." It was the truth and he must have seen it in her eyes.

"Good," he nodded, the hardness in him fading away on the instant as he turned to reach for another interesting tidbit. "I think I've still got the old shark instincts and talents."

Kalinda heard the wry satisfaction in his words and blinked, confused more than ever. "What's going on here, Rand? Are you telling me you were teasing me just then? That you were faking that...that threat?"

She put a hand on the sleeve of his jacket, urgently demanding his attention. His head swung back to her, the white teeth flashing in a reassuring grin that made her want to kick him.

"You believed me, didn't you?" he countered pointedly. "For a minute or two you thought me fully capable of blackmailing you into an affair."

"You sound proud of it!" she accused, cheeks

staining with annoyance and growing embarrass-
ment at her obvious gullibility.

The grin faded into a self-mocking grimace.
"No, I'm not proud of it. But it is a useful business
skill, I'm sorry to say."

"What's a useful business skill? Blackmail?"
she raged heatedly, having difficulty keeping her
voice down.

"The skill of being able to make people think
I'll stop at nothing when it comes to getting what
I want," he explained kindly, soothingly. "I just
wanted you to have a small demonstration so you
can introduce me to your..."

"Introduce you as what?" she gritted.

"The outside consultant you've hired to direct
the defenses of Brady Data Processing," he retorted
easily. He appeared about to add to that when his
glance went suddenly to a point beyond her head.
The hazel eyes gleamed warmly. "Hey, you really
did like the pot, huh?"

"Your conversation is getting more and more
difficult to follow," Kalinda muttered and turned to
follow his gaze. The lovely, wide-mouthed bowl
she had bought the first day in his gallery sat in a
prominent position at the far end of the table. It
held long loaves of sliced French bread which
guests had used to build small sandwiches.

He glanced down at her, looking enormously
pleased. "I'm glad you didn't try to forget me com-

pletely. I've still got a token of your short visit, too.''

''What token?'' she asked warily.

''The earrings I took off you that first night.''

''Oh.'' She'd forgotten about those.

''You shouldn't have run away that morning after we made love, sweetheart,'' he went on, dark voice turning slightly husky as he regarded her a little hungrily. ''Although I understand why you did.''

Kalinda flicked an uneasy glance up through her lashes. ''You do?''

''Of course. You thought there was no future for us, didn't you? You thought I wasn't the kind of man you should be giving yourself to so completely. And it was completely, honey. You came to my bed without any reservations, didn't you? For a little while you stopped thinking about the fact that I was an unmotivated, unambitious, undynamic wastrel who had no further goal in life except to fish and seduce bored tourists!''

Kalinda felt her blush deepening and she could no longer meet his eyes, even through the partial veil of her lashes. She remembered her unwise surrender only too well. What really worried her now was the flash of pure happiness she'd experienced when she'd opened her door a few minutes ago and found him standing there.

"You have to admit we do come from two different worlds, Rand," she managed a little grimly.

"Which is a polite way of saying you don't admire my lifestyle," he retorted dryly. "I'm here to change all that. I'm going to prove myself to you, sweetheart. And your ex-fiancé has put the tool I need right into my hands. You admire successful, dynamic, aggressive businessmen? Okay, I'll show you I can wheel and deal in your world with the best of them. Don't worry, Kalinda, you don't have to be ashamed of our affair. You'll be giving yourself to a man who can out-shark anyone on the business street!"

"Rand! This is crazy! I don't know what you're talking about, but I certainly have no intention of...of continuing what should never have been started up there in the mountains. I do not routinely indulge in affairs, for heaven's sake! I haven't been even remotely serious about any man since my engagement with David ended."

"Except me," he pointed out, smiling. "Or are you going to stand there and tell me you weren't perfectly serious that morning in the mountains?"

Kalinda glared at him, aware that he was deliberately goading her and still too confused and upset by the combination of the day's events to think clearly enough to flatten him verbally.

She was desperately trying to concoct a suitable response when Harold Sebastian and his wife emerged from the crowd with pleasantly expectant expressions.

"Kalinda, my dear, you must introduce us to your new guest." Tall, stately, and silver-haired, Harold beamed complacently down at her. While she was his superior at Brady Data Processing, his long association with her father had given him a decidedly paternalistic air toward the new president of the firm. It was an attitude Kalinda encountered from many of the longtime employees of the firm. They gave her their loyalty and even admired her ability, but they never quite let her forget they all considered themselves honorary uncles and aunts.

"I'm afraid my arrival was something of a surprise for Kalinda," Rand said smoothly, thrusting out a polite hand. "I'm Rand Alastair."

"Harold Sebastian. This is my wife, Edna," Harold said genially. "Alastair," he repeated with a thoughtful look. "That name sounds familiar. Have we met?"

"No, I don't believe so. But I can assure you the name is going to sound a lot more familiar in the future. I'm going to be working for Kalinda."

Kalinda froze as Harold's inquiring, interested gaze switched to her. "I see. In what capacity?"

"I'll, uh, be explaining Mr. Alastair's role to everyone tomorrow morning," she got out weakly, feeling trapped. "He will be with us in a very limited, short-term capacity,'' she added spitefully as Rand shot her an amused look.

"Well, well, I'll look forward to having you with us, Rand. You won't find a nicer boss in town!'' Harold assured him with a vast chuckle.

"Like father, like daughter,'' Edna Sebastian added warmly. "Everyone at the company is delighted that she took over the reins two years ago. Just ask anyone in the room!'' Edna waved gaily at the crowd behind them.

"I'm sure I shall thoroughly enjoy my association with her, also,'' Rand said glibly, his eyes still on Kalinda's studiously composed face.

He grinned down at her as the Sebastians faded back into the crowd. "You seemed to be well-liked by your staff,'' he drawled.

"It's positively feudal at times,'' she sighed, acknowledging the truth. "We're a publicly owned company but somehow everyone still thinks of it as a family firm.''

"How long ago did you go public with your stock?'' he asked, suddenly serious.

"Almost as soon as I took over. We needed capital and we needed it badly. I had to convince everyone that it was a clear turnaround situation, make investors think that they could get in on the ground floor of a company that was about to make a big comeback. I've never worked so hard in all my life!''

"I'll bet," he nodded assessingly. "The stock is now widely held?"

"Yes, I'm afraid so." She winced. "Not so long ago I was glad of that!"

"Now you realize that it just makes it easier for Hutton to buy up shares. You don't have any large controlling blocks sitting in friendly hands."

"You needn't look so superior. I had no choice at the time! I couldn't get the loans I needed from the banks. There was no choice but to raise capital by selling shares in the firm!"

"You don't have to defend your actions to me, sweetheart," he murmured caressingly. "I understand completely."

She fixed him with a narrow glance. "Just how much do you understand? Who are you, Rand? Why does Harold think he remembers your name? How do you come to have contacts high enough in the business world to find out what Hutton's doing even before I do?"

"It's a long story, honey. Remind me to tell it to you later. For now, though, I think we'd better circulate. People are beginning to notice that I'm getting your undivided attention!"

He put a hand firmly under her elbow and waded into the crowd. Kalinda felt herself helplessly swept along, her thoughts in a turmoil, her heart beating a little too fast and her nerves singing a tune on the

ragged edge of an emotion she didn't want to admit
to feeling.

But she knew how to deal with a crowd of business-oriented people. By the time the last of the
guests had regretfully taken his leave, Kalinda
would have been willing to wager that none of them
had guessed at her inner uncertainty and confusion.
She *was* aware, however, that more than one knowing glance had absorbed the fact that Rand seldom
left her side during the evening. She saw the assessing look in Colin Wayne's eyes although he
was cordial when he was introduced. Rand paid him
no particular attention, apparently oblivious to the
querying glance in the other man's gaze.

Kalinda was also conscious of the pleased speculation from the members of her own staff in the
crowd and the curious, smiling looks from others.
And some, like Harold, looked as if they could almost place Rand.

It seemed like forever before she gratefully
closed the door on the last guest and turned to see
Rand pouring himself a snifter of cognac. He had
drunk very little during the course of the evening
and he looked as if he were anticipating the nightcap with relish.

She watched grimly as he lowered himself into
an apricot chair and put up his feet. He saluted her
briefly with the glass in his hand.

"I must thank you for an interesting evening,

honey. I trust I didn't embarrass you with my un-sophisticated mountain manners?''

She started forward, not certain yet how she was going to deal with him but knowing she must handle matters firmly. ''You know very well you fit in as if you'd been in the business world all your adult life!''

He took a tentative sip of cognac as she came to a halt in front of him, his green-and-gold eyes laughing up at her.

''To the manner born,'' he intoned. ''Except for the past year and a half.''

She fit her hands to her hips, the silk dress soft beneath her fingers. ''I would like an explanation, Rand. Is that too much to ask?''

''I would like to go to bed with you. Is that too much to ask?''

The sudden lazy desire in his words stopped her for an instant. It also sidetracked her from her initial intent. Something far more immediately crucial was vibrating in the atmosphere between them.

She gathered her courage. ''You're not staying here tonight. I meant what I said. Last weekend was a mistake and I don't intend to repeat it.''

He surveyed her with a probing expression. ''A mistake? Do you really think of it that way?''

''Yes, dammit! I do!'' The protest was a little too vehement and Kalinda was aware of it.

''Come here and let me change your mind,'' he

offered deeply, extending invitingly upward to draw her down onto his lap.

Kalinda stepped away, trying vainly to cover her nervousness by scooping up a stack of glasses and heading for the kitchen. She knew he was following her, his footfalls soft on the thick green carpet.

She couldn't retreat any further than the sink. Just as she set the glasses down with a clink Rand came up behind her, his hands gliding possessively, longingly around her waist.

"I want you, sweetheart," he murmured, his breath warm on her hair. "More than I wanted you that morning in the mountains and at the time I didn't think anything could be stronger than that need."

"Oh, Rand, please don't do this to me! I don't want an affair. I don't want to be one of your weekend women...."

"There won't be any other women, Kalinda," he promised with absolute conviction, his fingers sliding up to cup her breasts. "You are the only one I want. Why do you think I followed you back to Denver? What we found together was very special, sweetheart. Can't you at least admit that much?"

She trembled as his lips touched the back of her neck. He kissed her nape and the curve of her shoulder as his fingertips gently circled the tips of her breasts through the material of the silk. She felt the need and want in him and it was like a drug, stirring her own responses even while she desperately tried to talk herself into a rational course of action.

"We…we had something very short and meaningless…."

"Meaningless!" He swung her around to face him, a raw, demanding look on his face. "I'll grant it was a little *short,*" he said tightly, "but it sure as hell wasn't meaningless! At least," he went on accusingly, "not to me. Are you trying to tell me you were using me, Kalinda? That you only came by my house on your way out of town to conclude a weekend fling with a man who amused you?"

"Don't put words in my mouth! You know it wasn't like that!"

Anxiously she frowned up at him, her fingers splayed across the finely woven material of his suit jacket. "I…I felt I had to see you again to tell you that you had succeeded in making me see reason where David was concerned. You were so worried about me."

"With good reason, as it turned out. The man's trying to destroy you!"

"But I never intended to go to bed with you!"

"Then why did you?" he countered with the trace of a smile.

"Because…because…" She broke off, floundering for an explanation of the unexplainable.

"Because you wanted me as much as I wanted

you," he finished for her, all sure, masculine triumph as he pulled her close. "And I'm going to see if I can't make you want me even more in the days to come. Starting tonight."

"No! All you want from me is sex. I won't fall into that trap," she cried as he lowered his head to take her lips.

"You're wrong, honey," he whispered seductively against her mouth. "I want something much more important from you. I want a commitment."

Kalinda struggled. Struggled to ask him what he meant by a commitment, struggled to free herself from his embrace. Both efforts failed abysmally as his kiss swamped her senses.

Just as it had that morning in his home by the lake, the potent desire in him reached out to trap her senses and send them reeling. It fed the desire in herself until Kalinda could barely sustain the futile struggle to control it.

He seemed oblivious of her hands pushing on his shoulders, his hold on her a warm, confining, unshakable thing that kept her gently, securely in his grasp. It lured her, seduced her, promised the stars to her and her traitorous body believed everything.

He groaned with relief and longing as he coaxed apart her lips, feeling them soften and yield beneath his own. His hands slid down her back, urging her body more firmly against tautening thighs.

Kalinda felt herself sinking against him, responding to his passion with a desperate craving of her own. A craving she had never known before she had met this man who mystified her. Reality spun away, leaving only the knowledge that he was here with her again. The emptiness she had experienced as she drove away from him that morning in the mountains was at last being filled.

His tongue, moving with hot aggression in her mouth, slowly withdrew as Rand gently, reluctantly broke the kiss.

"Take me into your bed, Kalinda. I swear I'll be as loyal as any of your faithful band of employees. I'll keep the marauding sharks away from your door for you."

She turned her head into his shoulder, felt his damp, arousing kisses on the vulnerable, sensitized skin behind her ear and then on her throat.

"I thought it was yourself you called a shark," she reminded him shakily, trying to think straight and knowing it was hopeless.

"It takes one to fight one, sweetheart." He trembled against her, eliciting that seductive feeling of female power that she had known before with him. It was power combined with the illogical desire to satisfy. It made no sense to Kalinda but it seemed to make perfect sense to her body.

"Are you really a shark?" she whispered, tipping her head back to meet his eyes searchingly.

He sucked in his breath, his hands tightening around her waist.

"Yes," he said with heavy honesty. "But you can control me, darling. I'll only work for you, never against you. Please believe me!"

She shook her head, dazed. "But I don't understand, Rand. If you know all about the ruthless side of the business world, if you have those abilities, what were you doing for the past year and a half in the mountains?"

He hesitated, as if uncertain how to explain himself. "I was running away from what those abilities had made me. I was running away from the shark I had become. A year and a half ago I took a good look at myself, sweetheart, and decided I didn't like what I saw. I needed time to think, time to discover another side of life. So I went to the mountains."

Kalinda saw the naked, vulnerable look in his eyes and knew in that moment that he'd never told another soul what he'd just told her. Before she could stop to think, she lifted her palms to either side of his harshly carved face.

"And now you think you want to come back to the life you left behind? What makes you believe it will be any different this time, Rand?"

"This time I have you. This time I have something more important than building an empire."

In spite of the tension of the moment, Kalinda's

lips twitched. "I'm supposed to be a civilizing influence on a shark?"

"I seem," he observed, sweeping her up into his arms with an easy movement, "to be fated to serve as a source of amusement for you!"

"I wasn't laughing at you," she protested, clinging automatically as he began striding out of the kitchen.

"Yes, you were," he said beguilingly. "But I know how to wipe that smile out of your lovely eyes!"

When he turned unerringly down the hall to her bedroom, Kalinda's head fell back against his shoulder, her lashes drooping softly to flicker on her cheeks.

Her implicit surrender made itself felt. Rand held her with fierce passion as he walked into the bedroom at the end of the hall. With a glance around the room, he made his way to the bed and settled her gently down on it.

The green and apricot color scheme had been reversed in this room; the apricot in the carpet, the verdant green in the bedspread and chair. In her red and gold and peacock blue silk, Kalinda was a splash of vibrant color as she lay on the green spread.

"You look like some exotic creature from a harem lying there waiting for me." Rand stood beside the bed, pulling free the satin bow tie and dropping it onto the carpet.

"Your harem?" she asked throatily, her gaze trapped by his.

"Definitely," he smiled, his fingers on the buttons of his white shirt. "But it's a harem of one."

Kalinda felt herself melting beneath the heat of his gaze and when he had finished undressing himself and reached for her, she shivered violently with the emotion his touch aroused.

"Kalinda, my gentle, passionate Kalinda," he rasped, pulling her into his arms and finding the fastenings of her dress with fingers that shook ever so slightly. "I couldn't believe you had left me when I awoke that morning. I couldn't believe you hadn't found in my arms what I had found in yours. You credited me with good perception but you were wrong. I would never have guessed you would have left like that...."

"I saw so little future for us." She stirred as the coolness in the room bathed her skin. He removed her dress with deftness and a sensual touch that was a caress in itself. She lifted appealing eyes to his intent face. "And I'm not sure there's any more of a future now than there was before. Why *did* you follow me, Rand?"

"Hush, darling," he whispered, bending to kiss the nipple of her breast as it hardened beneath his hand. "Stop trying to put obstacles in our path. We need each other tonight. Let that be enough for the time being.''

Under his possessive, exploring touch, Kalinda had no choice but to put the doubts and fears aside. What he offered at that moment was too important, too wonderful to turn down. And he knew it. He was using that fact to seduce her as surely as he used his lips and fingers and the strength of his hard, lean body.

Cradling her against him, Rand rested on one elbow, his free hand trailing exciting patterns down the length of her side to her thighs. He felt her response and slowly built the tempo of the random patterns until she moaned and turned her mouth into his chest.

Finding the male nipples with her quick, gentle teeth, Kalinda returned the mounting excitement, glorifying in his reaction. She felt him shift his legs, inserting one foot between her own. Then his circling, feathering hand went to the inside of her thighs.

''Oh!'' The sob of desire was muffled against his skin but he heard it and growled her name against her shoulder.

''My God, Kalinda, you make me wonder how I ever got along without you in my bed!''

She raked her nails convulsively but lightly along his back, down to the sensitive point at the base of his spine and beyond. He arched into her, his hand moving exquisitely at the point where her thighs joined her body.

She felt the arousing, passionate sensations take her beyond the edge of reasoning thought. All that mattered was Rand. She wondered how she could ever have survived without knowing this powerful emotion again. In the back of her mind, Kalinda acknowledged the truth. She would have eventually gone back to the mountains looking for him.

"I would have come back, Rand," she confessed huskily. "I told myself I had to get over you, that there was no future for us. But I know now I would have come back."

Gently he turned her on her back, his leg thrown heavily across hers. "I couldn't wait, sweetheart. I had to follow you. I had to know if I could make you need me as badly as I needed you!"

He strung fiery little kisses all down her throat, across her soft breasts and along the curve of her stomach. She surged beneath his questing hands, unable to hide her desire.

"Do you have any idea what it does to me when you ignite like this in my arms? I couldn't stand the thought of you coming back to Denver and finding someone else! You're mine, Kalinda. I made you mine last weekend. I swear you'll find me worthy of your sweet surrender."

Kalinda gasped at his progressively intimate demands, her eyes tightly shut as her head fell back over his outstretched arm. "Such a risk, it's such a risk...."

"No," he whispered forcefully. "I'll take care of everything. You don't have to worry about getting pregnant!"

And Kalinda, who had been too far gone in the dazzling world of sensation he had created to even think about that particular risk, gave up trying to tell him her real fears.

He soothed her body with his hands and lips, finding the secret places he had discovered once before and reforging the bond he'd created then. Even as he made love to her, tuning her body to his, Kalinda realized the strength of the link he had bound her with that morning in the mountains.

He knew her so well, she thought wonderingly. She had called him perceptive, but even she hadn't realized the depths of that perception. He had known he could show up on her doorstep tonight and reweave the magic they had found once before.

Her own instincts had been more confused on the issue but under the impact of his desire they homed in on the truth.

When she thought she could stand no more of the teasing, exhilarating lovemaking, when she thought it must surely drive her insane if he didn't stake the final claim, Rand came to her with a fierce and gentle power that left her no option but to respond in kind.

In the darkness she clung to him as she had that morning by the lake, knowing an almost violent satisfaction at the knowledge that this time she couldn't run away when it was over.

The driving force of his need took them both into a timeless world of sensuality that left no room for the unbidden questions a portion of Kalinda's mind still asked.

Seven

Kalinda awoke the next morning with a curious sense of expectancy. She sensed the missing weight beside her in the bed and turned her tousled head on the pillow. At the same moment that she registered the empty place where Rand had been she realized the shower was going full blast.

She lay perfectly still for a moment, letting the memories of last night's passion and intimacy wash over her. Again and again in the darkness Rand had reached for her, pulling her close, telling her of his need.

And she had gone to him, refusing to think of the future, allowing only her woman's need to satisfy and be satisfied to guide her.

In the morning light, Kalinda lay gazing across the expanse of apricot carpet and asked herself the question she hadn't wanted to ask during the night.

Why had Rand followed her back to Denver? It was hard to believe that he wanted an affair so badly he felt obliged to "prove" himself worthy of her regard. He didn't strike her as the sort of man who had ever felt it necessary to prove himself to anyone.

He must have met and probably seduced any number of tourists, she thought wretchedly, flinging back the covers. But how many had he followed back to Denver, seeking an affair?

But if it was routine for him, it was not routine for her. Kalinda had not been seriously interested in anyone after David Hutton had taken back his ring. There had been two reasons for maintaining the most casual of relationships. One had been the necessity for almost complete attention to Brady Data Processing. She had always been a hard worker, but the effort to save the company had required a ceaseless effort for the first couple of years. And memories of the fool she had been for trusting in David had constituted the second reason for extreme caution in her associations with men.

Yet within two days of knowing Rand Alastair she had gone to bed with him, and when he had shown up on her doorstep last night, she had known the probable result. Known it and put up very little argument against it.

Kalinda got to her feet and winced at the unexpected soreness in her muscles. The evidence of the intensity of Rand's lovemaking was going to be undeniable for a day or two, she thought dryly, reaching for a soft velour robe and belting it firmly around her waist.

She took a deep, steadying breath and headed for the bathroom where it sounded as if Rand was going through her hot water in record time. It was as she tentatively opened the door, the steam hitting her full in the face, that she realized she didn't know exactly what she was going to say.

But something had to be said, she told herself resolutely. Last night had been only the beginning of an affair as far as Rand was concerned, but for her it had brought the blinding realization that she was in love with the man.

She didn't want to be. Kalinda had no real desire to be in love with anyone. The last time she had allowed her emotions to become vulnerable she had been made to look a fool. Yet two years later she found herself swept into a far more passionate situation than she had ever known with David and with a man she barely knew.

How even as she stood there in the bathroom doorway letting the steam escape Kalinda recognized the depths of her feelings for the man standing complacently under her shower. She had let him in last night because she had taken one look at him and realized the strength of the bonds he had forged that morning in the mountains. She had gone to bed with him last night and let him strengthen those intimate bonds until by morning she had no alternative but to acknowledge them.

"Come on in and close the door, you're letting all the heat out!" Rand called from behind the shower curtain. "About time you got up. I was just about to come in and wake you!" He stuck his head around the curtain, water plastering the chestnut hair to his head, the hazel eyes gleaming with remembered satisfaction as he took in her robe-covered figure.

Kalinda found herself responding to his obvious good mood in spite of her newfound resolution to have a serious talk. "Were you going to wait until you'd used up all the hot water before you called me?"

"I've been saving some for you," he retorted imperturbably. "Come on in."

"I'll wait," she declared firmly. "Rand, I want to talk to you…"

"Come a little closer, it's hard to hear over the noise of the water," he remarked innocently, ducking back behind the shower.

Uncertainly Kalinda moved forward. "I suppose it can wait until you're finished," she began and then belatedly tried to step backward as a long, wet arm darted out to snag her waist. An instant later he reappeared from behind the curtain, a teasing grin slashing his tanned face.

"Come on in, honey. The water's fine."

"Rand, this is serious," she began earnestly and then had to stop her argument in order to push away his fingers as they reached for the belt on the robe. "I need to talk to you."

"I'm listening." He pulled her closer, slipping the robe off her shoulders and, still holding her, plunking the green shower cap down on her head. "You look cute this morning," he murmured, surveying her with a satisfied nod. "Rather like a grumpy cat."

"Are you always in such a lively mood at this hour of the day?" she demanded caustically as he tugged her into the stall beside him. The full force of the water struck her and she found it pleasantly reviving in spite of her mood.

"You'll have a chance to do a statistical analysis on the subject and find out, won't you?" Rand reached for the soap and, cradling her with one arm against his slippery side, began to lather her back.

"That's...that's what I wanted to talk to you about," she said breathlessly, violently aware of the uncompromising maleness of him. It was entirely disconcerting to have him taking over her bathroom and her life and Kalinda fought for a means of self-defense.

"First my good-morning kiss," he intoned, bending his head to find her lips as his hand slid possessively down her back and over the curve of her hip.

"Rand, please listen to me. This is very serious...."

"Ummm," he growled against her mouth, tasting her with evident enjoyment. "Just what a man needs to get the day started properly!"

Beneath the warm water streaming over them his mouth moved even more warmly over hers, probing deeply, lazily, possessively. Kalinda found herself clutching his glistening shoulders, aware of just how much he was telling her with this proprietary good-morning kiss. It was very clear that as far as Rand Alastair was concerned, she was now his. Kalinda wasn't sure how to argue with that overwhelming assumption, especially since her whole being longed to agree.

The hand on her hip began gliding upward, fingers spreading briefly across her stomach before continuing the journey to her breasts. He caressed her with slick, sensuous motions that made her tremble against him.

But when she unconsciously moaned a throaty response and moved her own hand down to his waist and beyond, it was Rand who lifted his head and turned her firmly around to break the contact.

"Enough of that wantonness, Miss Brady. You and I have work to do today," he chided bracingly. "None of which is going to get done if you seduce me here in the shower!"

"I wasn't seducing you," she began wrathfully, feeling the laughter in him. "I was the innocent victim!"

"It's all in one's point of view, I suppose," he shrugged philosophically. "Now, what was it you had to tell me?" Briskly he finished soaping her body.

"I'll...I'll tell you during breakfast," she sighed. Then she realized there had been no scrape of morning beard when he had kissed her. "How did you manage a shave?"

"I had my things downstairs in the car. I threw on my slacks and went down to get them before you awoke."

"You really came prepared, didn't you?" she muttered.

"A man has to look his best first day on a new job."

"You meant what you said last night? You're really going to help my company fight off David's takeover bid?" she asked uncertainly.

"Don't worry, honey. One way or another I'll see to it Hutton doesn't get the firm."

It was only later over the breakfast of scrambled eggs and toast she prepared that Kalinda finally found the courage to bring up the subject which had been on her mind since she awoke.

"Where did you plan on staying while you're in Denver, Rand?" She didn't meet his eyes as she set the plates down on the table.

There was a heavy pause from the other side of the table. Unwillingly Kalinda finally looked up from her eggs. Rand was regarding her with a rather enigmatic speculation.

"Is this the opening volley in your small war to make sure I don't stay here with you?"

She held onto her determination. "I think that as long as you're intent on working for Brady we ought to maintain a...a more businesslike association."

"I'm supposed to prove myself worthy of the affair before you'll continue with it?" he murmured mildly.

"I'm not asking you to prove anything, Rand. You're the one who showed up unannounced on my doorstep last night in the middle of a party and said you were coming to work for me!" she flared.

"I didn't come back to Denver only to work for you."

Kalinda felt herself go warm under the caressing glance he poured over her. "Do you always follow your latest female interest in order to pursue an affair?'' she whispered.

"I haven't been out of those mountains for eighteen months,'' he said evenly.

"Then why have you come after me?'' she managed tightly.

His face gentled. "I thought I made that obvious last night.''

She shook her head. "Rand, we knew each other for only a couple of days....''

The edge of his mouth turned upward and he said carelessly, "As you are soon going to learn, I am nothing if not a first-rate strategist and decision-maker. I know what I want, Kalinda.''

"And you think you want me?''

"I know I want you. I also want to show you I'm fully capable of the business skills you seem to admire so greatly. I saw the disapproval in your eyes when you commented on my rather easygoing way of life in the mountains. You admire men from your own world. So I'm going to show you I can handle myself in that world.''

"There's no need...''

"There's every need. But if it will make you less fretful this morning I'll tell you I have a place to stay. You don't have to worry about giving me room and board.'' He dug into his eggs with gusto.

"Where?'' she asked, wishing it didn't seem so right having him here sitting across from her at breakfast. But she had to know more about him, more about his motives. She simply could not believe he had followed her just to take her to bed again.

"An apartment here in town," he smiled. "Now eat your breakfast, sweetheart, we have a lot to do today."

It wasn't until later that morning when Kalinda convened an emergency meeting of the highest-ranking members of her staff that she realized she wasn't the only one with a profound wariness of Rand Alastair's motives.

But the hard chill in the air that greeted her as she walked into the conference room with Rand at her side took Kalinda by surprise. She was accustomed to an easy, comfortable, respectful familiarity from the circle of mostly middle-aged faces. The shock of the cold nervousness she saw in even Harold Sebastian's eyes left her momentarily unnerved.

Rand seemed totally unaffected by it, taking a seat with a casual nod to the ring of eyes that focused on him. Then he politely turned his attention to Kalinda and she automatically took control.

"What I have to say will be a shock for all of you," she began grimly, glancing around the table. "But perhaps that's my fault. I should have anticipated such an event, given the current merger fever in this country. To put it bluntly, Brady Data Processing has become the target company of a hostile bid…''

The rumble of stunned, accusing voices interrupted her. Before Kalinda could recall the meeting to order, she realized that Rand was the focus of the grim glances and angry murmurs. He sat unheeding, his eyes on Kalinda.

"If I may have your attention," she said dryly, still not fully comprehending the reaction of her staff. Why were they staring at Rand like that?

"You'll have to understand, Miss Brady," Palmer Greyson said finally, his portly body rigid with indignation. "We're all a little stunned by this. When Harold told us this morning that you'd been seen on friendly terms with Rand Alastair, well, we just couldn't believe it. How could you? Your father would never have done such a thing. I'm sure he would be as shocked as the rest of us to know you…''

"I assure you, Palmer," Kalinda said, appalled, "the takeover attempt is not my idea. I believe I mentioned the bid being made is a hostile one!"

"But Harold said you were more than a little friendly with Alastair last night and others saw you…''

Kalinda, realizing the drawbacks to running business in a more or less democratic way, tightened her mouth and regarded her accusers coolly.

"I'm sorry to have to admit it, but, frankly, I

don't have the skills necessary to combat the bid. And neither, if you're honest with yourselves, do any of you! We have gone our own way here at Brady, staying out of the conglomeration movement and concentrating on building our firm from within. As a result, we've allowed ourselves to be taken by surprise...."

"You can't just turn the company over to him without a fight!" Harold Sebastian interrupted forcefully, bringing his hand down flatly on the table. He swung his head around to stare at Rand who merely arched an eyebrow in response. "I knew your name was familiar last night but it took me until this morning to place it. How did you talk Kalinda into this? She's always been as concerned with Brady as her father was...."

"That's enough, Harold," Kalinda said quietly, the authority in her voice bringing all eyes back to her. "There seems to be some misunderstanding here. If you know something I don't know then perhaps you should tell me about it. In the meantime, hear me out. We will then throw the subject open for discussion. Is that agreeable?"

With muttered remarks and a few resentful glances at Rand Kalinda's staff settled back into their seats, clearly expecting to hear nothing hopeful from her.

"We need an expert. Mr. Alastair claims competence in the specialized area of business we need at this moment. With your approval I intend to hire him to advise us during the next few weeks.''

"Hire him!" The startled exclamation was repeated around the table as everyone turned to stare uncomprehendingly at everyone else. Only Rand remained aloof, looking half-amused.

"Yes, unless, as I noted earlier, you have some serious objection or a better suggestion," Kalinda finished forcefully.

"Miss Brady," Margaret Vannon said very slowly, her graying blond hair still an attractive frame for her pleasant features. "Who, exactly, is proposing to take over Brady?"

She told them the name of David Hutton's firm and saw the astonishment in their faces.

"Hutton is trying to force a merger on us?" Harold asked a little blankly, staring at Rand again. "Not Alastair?"

It was Kalinda's turn to look blank. "That's correct."

"And you're proposing to hire Rand Alastair? To have him on our side?" Palmer Greyson said in wondering disbelief.

"Yes. Now I'm prepared to throw this discussion onto the table, although it already appears to be there," she noted dryly. "I'm quite willing to have your input since this affects all of us. Hutton, by the way, has already filed with the SEC. We're running out of time. May I have your comments, please? Perhaps you would like to question Rand on his qualifications.''

"His qualifications!" Margaret Vannon echoed wryly. "They could hardly be any better, as I'm sure you know." She looked frankly at Rand. "Have you really agreed to help Brady in this matter?''

Rand inclined his head in silent agreement.

"You'll be working for us?''

"Yes," he smiled politely.

There was a thoughtful silence while everyone absorbed this. Kalinda was still trying to figure out what her staff knew about Rand that she didn't when the vice-president in charge of marketing said half-humorously, "How's it going to feel being on the other side of the action, Mr. Alastair?''

"Interesting," Rand replied, a small, anticipatory grin on his lips.

As if the single word had removed a barrier, the questions started coming fast and furiously. But this time they were asked with a growing excitement and confidence that told Kalinda the turning point had been reached.

Rand had gone from being the villain at the table to the hero. She didn't understand it but she was too good a businesswoman to question her luck. Her staff's obvious confidence in Rand's abilities reinforced her own decision to believe in him. She sat musingly and watched him handle the questions and comments with easy skill. He really did know what he was doing. And he appeared familiar with the respect he was receiving. Yes, she thought privately, she had a lot of questions for Rand Alastair.

But it was Harold Sebastian who answered many of them for her. He approached her as the meeting broke up sometime later, an apologetic smile on his now-pleased face.

"You've really pulled off a coup, Kalinda. Your father would have been proud of you. Alastair may have been maintaining a low profile for the past couple of years but there's no doubt he's still got the ability! I'll admit when I finally remembered who he was this morning and realized just how friendly the two of you seemed last night, I had a few bad moments. So did everyone else. That man's reputation alone might be enough to spike David Hutton's guns! How did you ever persuade Alastair to come back into battle? Word had it he'd retired a couple of years ago."

"Just what is his reputation, Harold?" Kalinda asked ruefully. "I mean, he's admitted he knows something about the conglomeration business, but..."

"Knows something about it! My God, Kalinda, that man was the terror of every firm in the Rockies up until about two years ago. He had a reputation as a corporate raider that made Genghis Khan look tame! He had a piece of the action wherever he wanted it. Sometimes he would force a takeover, sometimes he only wanted a seat on the board of a particular firm. He manipulated stock, added any firm that took his eye to his own conglomerate, and generally seemed unstoppable. It got to the point where the mere mention that he was interested in a company was enough to send the management into panic.''

''How is it I never heard of him?''

''The timing, I suppose. You were working at that firm in Houston until about three months before your father was killed. You got engaged, as I recall, shortly after you moved up here from Texas. Alastair was going into retirement about the time you were going through the shock of your father's death. When I saw you walk in with Alastair this morning I knew we were headed for disaster. And then when you said we were a target company...''

''You saw Rand sitting there and assumed I'd just handed over the reins to a shark?'' Kalinda mused with a wry smile.

''I should have known you'd never do anything like that. I guess I panicked, too, just the way everyone used to do when they heard Alastair was coming!'' Harold grinned. ''But to have him actually working for us...!''

''You don't mind having a shark around as long as he's on your side?''

''Business is business,'' Harold chuckled and

then excused himself to hurry off to his office. Rand had already begun dispatching people for the various reports and records he wanted to see.

The management offices of Brady Data Processing took on the atmosphere of an armed camp preparing for battle. Word went like wildfire through the company of the takeover bid, but word of Rand's presence spread equally as fast. Instead of the sudden depression in morale, Kalinda was amazed to find everyone invigorated with a purposefulness that told its own story. Brady management had a battlefield general and they were prepared to follow him into the fray, no questions asked. There was nothing like having a shark on your side, Kalinda thought idly at one point when George Barrett appeared with coffee and sandwiches.

"Thanks, George," Kalinda smiled gratefully, looking up from the pile of papers on her desk. Rand, sitting across from her glanced up almost curiously and then looked appreciatively at the sandwiches.

"I didn't know an order for food had gone out," he grinned, helping himself to a thick pastrami on rye.

George lifted an eyebrow. "Miss Brady would never think to send me out for sandwiches," he murmured. "She respects my professionalism far too much, even in a crisis, to do such a thing. But

I have eyes and it was clear neither of you had remembered lunch today!''

He left the room with a stack of rough drafts that needed typing, all business. Rand watched him go, one brow cocked bemusedly.

''Things seem to have changed in the business world during the past couple of years,'' was his only comment.

''George is the perfect secretary,'' Kalinda said calmly, watching his expression.

''Bosses,'' Rand drawled, ''are known for falling in love with their secretaries.''

''George would never allow such an improper situation to develop,'' Kalinda said blandly. ''Here's that breakdown on Brady's line of credit you requested.''

Most of the management staff stayed late that day, but not as late as Kalinda and Rand. The ultimate responsibility was on their shoulders and Kalinda found her new employee seemed avid to accept his share. It was, she decided, as if the shark had swum back into his element. An impressive sight.

The dinner hour came and went, sandwiches and coffee once again the only fare. After the brief break during which Rand asked a series of probing questions concerning the material he'd been going through they both plunged back into the task of planning the defense strategy. Rand was intent on immersing himself in a thorough understanding of Brady's resources, weaknesses, and possible options.

Finally, shortly after ten o'clock he closed the manila folder in front of him and got to his feet. "Come on, honey, let's go home. We're not going to be worth a damn tomorrow if we don't get some sleep tonight."

"Where is your apartment, Rand?" Kalinda asked bravely, rising to her feet and stretching as a yawn threatened. She must be firm.

"I'm going to show you," he smiled benignly.

"I meant what I said this morning," she began determinedly. "I think we ought to maintain a business relationship until we have a chance to know each other better."

"I said I'd show you the apartment, I didn't promise to seduce you, too." He gathered up a stack of papers and shoved them into a leather case. "I'm not even sure I could at this stage," he reflected seriously. "It's been a while since I worked like this. I'm a little out of shape!"

She smiled at that. "You don't look it. You look like an eager warhorse getting back into harness!"

He took her arm and walked her toward the door. "Nevertheless, the stamina requirements are a trifle different than those of fishing and pottery-making!"

The white Lotus sped through the night toward an elegant apartment building near the downtown area. It was not far from her own town house, she thought ruefully.

"Come on up for a nightcap. We deserve it," Rand instructed, giving her little option as he took her arm once again and assisted her out of the car.

"How do you happen to have an apartment, Rand?" she murmured, trying not to think of the decision which lay ahead of her tonight. How could she refuse him if he made love to her? His touch was like magic on her skin and the warmth in him was almost irresistible. She loved the man. But she had to have the answers to her questions about him. No amount of logic could convince her he had followed her out of the mountains merely for an affair. And he'd said nothing of love....

"I own the building," he confessed.

"Own it!"

"It was one of the few things I hung onto when I opted out a year and a half ago," he explained, watching her face as he pushed the elevator button. "It was something that didn't have to be managed in person and provided a nice income."

She shook her head. "You're proving to be one surprise after another."

"Good surprises, I trust," he smiled.

"Are you so very concerned about my opinion?" she breathed, stepping into the elevator.

"I prefer seeing respect in your eyes rather than disapproval. Is that so strange?" he asked wistfully.

Kalinda could think of nothing to say to that. But some instinct warned her that a man like Rand Alastair didn't worry much about other people's opinions.

A moment later the elevator opened and they emerged into a thickly carpeted hallway. Rand fished a key out of his pocket and paused before the only door in sight.

"I phoned ahead and had the place put in order," he began as he opened the door. "I hope it's decent."

He flipped on the light, revealing a clean, uncluttered room furnished in an utterly masculine style. It was similar to the décor in his house by the lake, Kalinda thought, walking inside curiously. Browns and caramels were the predominant colors of the low-slung, modern furniture. Wide, sweeping vistas of the Denver night were provided by an expanse of windows.

Automatically Kalinda walked toward the view, knowing he was watching her. "It's lovely," she smiled, looking out into the darkness and picking out familiar buildings. They were on the twentieth floor.

"I prefer your place," he said dryly.

She swung around to see him going over to a liquor cabinet and begin hunting through the collection of bottles.

She accepted the snifter he held out to her a moment later, meeting his eyes silently over the rim as they each lifted their glasses. For an instant as she met the glittering promise in the hazel eyes, Kalinda forgot all about her promise to herself. And when he took her wrist and led her silently across the tan carpet to the sofa, she couldn't find the words of protest.

He sank down onto the leather cushions, tugging her gently down beside him. Then, wrapping the arm holding his drink around her shoulders so that she was forced to curl into his side, Rand reached for the leather case he brought with him.

He put his feet up on a hassock and fumbled briefly in the case. "Now, I've got a couple more questions about your relationship with the banks," he said calmly.

Kalinda turned her head quickly to stare at him and saw that he was quite serious. He didn't appear to have any intention of trying to seduce her tonight. She honestly didn't know whether to be glad or feel insulted.

The amusement lit her eyes and quirked her mouth as she dutifully answered his precise questions.

Half an hour later she was still answering the occasional question as Rand continued reading beside her. With a strange feeling of contentment she settled more closely against him, finding his obvious interest in the work at hand somehow endearing. He was enjoying this, she thought sleepily.

Her eyes were closing when the impact of that statement finally made itself felt.

He *was* enjoying himself! He was thriving on the opportunity to get back into the dangerous game he knew so well. Belatedly Kalinda remembered the occasional feeling she'd had in the mountains that he'd latched onto her because he had been as bored as she was up there.

She was almost asleep when the plausible answer to all her questions popped into her head.

Had Rand followed her back out of the mountains because she had made him realize he was bored with the easy life? Was he using her to find his way back to the high-powered business world he'd once dominated?

The thought of serving as an accidental catalyst for a man who once again was seeking a change of lifestyle was not a pleasant one. What happened to the catalyst after it had served its purpose?

Eight

Kalinda awoke hours later to find dawn pearling the sky outside the massive windows. She blinked, stirred warmly and finally opened her eyes to find herself wedged between the back of the sofa and Rand's lean frame.

They were still wearing their business suits, she realized, minus the jackets. Her camel shirt and white, bow-tie blouse would never be the same. Sometime during the night Rand had located a blanket and pulled it over both of them before going to sleep himself. Kalinda shifted position carefully and found herself snugly cradled, Rand's arm firmly wrapped around her.

She managed to prop herself on one elbow, desperate to stretch cramped muscles. Her hair was hanging loosely around her shoulders and she felt terribly mussed and sleep-tousled.

In the pale morning light Rand's firmly etched features appeared more relaxed. There was an unmistakable contentment in the eased lines around his mouth and eyes. His shirt had been undone at the collar, tie removed.

For a long moment Kalinda stared down at him, absorbing each detail along with the fact that she loved him. That look of contentment, she now realized, wasn't because he'd spent the night by her side. It was because Rand Alastair was finally back where he wanted to be. He had emerged from his year and a half of retirement to resume the fast-paced, perilous life he had known before opting out of the business world.

For how long would he see Kalinda as his means of getting back into the high-powered atmosphere he'd once dominated? Helping Brady Data Processing fight off a hostile merger attempt could only be a stepping-stone for such a man. Kalinda might have been the one to galvanize him into realizing he was bored with retirement, but how long would she hold his interest once the transition back to the business world had been made?

If her time with Rand was fated to be short-lived, why was she telling herself that she must control the passion in the relationship? Why shouldn't she be taking advantage of the precious, stolen moments? With luck she might have weeks, perhaps even a few months before he got swept up completely in the world he'd left behind. But it was already going to be incredibly difficult to say goodbye. How much worse would it be if the affair went on for months? The thought of watching Rand grow bored with her was frightening.

She was staring at him, wondering unhappily how she would explain her feelings to Rand when the chestnut lashes flickered against his cheekbones and lifted. The hazel gaze gleamed at her with sleepy contentment.

"Good morning, Miss Brady," he growled lazily, moving the hand that cradled her up to snag luxuriously in her hair. "You have an interesting way of conducting late-night business conferences. Do you always go to sleep in the middle of them?"

"I don't appear to be the only one who dozed off at this particular conference," she replied, warming under the possessiveness in his gaze. "Perhaps you should serve coffee instead of cognac when you conduct your late meetings."

"My only regret," he murmured, his mouth quirking with an intimate, teasing expression, "is the unfinished business we failed to get through."

Kalinda knew her cheeks were reddening under the complacent, very male look in his eyes. But before she could frame a properly light retort, the hand in her hair was moving to urge her head down to his.

With a muffled sigh Kalinda let herself be pulled across Rand's chest, her hair tumbling over his shoulders as he kissed her with slow satisfaction.

"I think we've got time to tie up a few loose ends," he whispered against her mouth.

Kalinda tried to take a firm grip on her new resolutions. "I agree," she said lightly and saw the pleased look on his face. "And I think an early-morning walk would be just the way to do it."

"A walk!"

"Ummm. A little exercise to get us revitalized for the new day."

"If it's exercise you're after, I have a better suggestion," he began determinedly, sliding his fingers up her throat and encircling the nape of her neck.

Kalinda resisted the temptation and the want in him with every atom of restraint she possessed. She had to start drawing the line. She had to ease out of this relationship before it became impossible to do so.

"Consider this little suggestion of mine as an order from your boss," she said, easing herself to a sitting position beside him.

He regarded her with a measure of fascination. "I'm not accustomed to taking orders," he finally pointed out.

"As you said yesterday, things have changed a bit in the business world since you opted out a year and a half ago!"

"Some things are basic. They never change." He reached for her.

"I'm serious, Rand," she said quietly, evading his arm. "I want to go for a walk. We…we need to talk."

He hesitated, as if testing the determination in her and then he shrugged eloquently. "Okay, boss, if that's really what you want."

They must have made a rather strange sight, Kalinda decided later as they walked briskly along the path of a nearby park. It was one of many such islands strung throughout the city. There were more than one hundred and fifty parks in Denver and Kalinda would have been willing to bet that few of them were being used at this hour of the morning by a couple dressed in business suits that had recently been slept in.

But it was invigorating. The beginning of a Colorado summer day shone down on them and to the west the mountains seemed to hold out the same promise they had for generations.

"Do you do this a lot?" Rand grinned wryly, clasping her hand as they walked.

"Of course not. I'd be afraid of getting mugged!"

"You think I can protect you?" he asked, slanting her an interested glance.

"If anyone dares menace us we'll just tell him who you are and use your reputation to scare him off!"

He winced. "That took you by surprise yesterday, didn't it?"

"Your reputation? Frankly, yes," Kalinda said simply, inhaling the morning air. "I'm told you really were the shark you joked about being that night at the party."

"Does that worry you?" he asked with surprising hesitation, not looking at her.

"Should it?"

"No. It's supposed to convince you I'm the sort of man you admire," he said softly.

"Which brings us to the subject I wanted to discuss," Kalinda said, amazed at the calm in her voice.

"I had a feeling it might," he sighed. "What's wrong, Kalinda?" His fingers tightened around hers, as if he were preparing for physical struggle.

"There's nothing wrong, Rand. I just want to make it clear that I meant what I said yesterday morning about maintaining...a businesslike relationship for a while. There's a lot we have to learn about each other...."

"You were upset about finding out about my past, weren't you?" he interrupted harshly. "But, honey, it's that past which is going to help your company. Don't you see?''

"I see. And I'm grateful. But that's not the point." She tried to speak rationally, keeping her emotions under control. But it was difficult with him looking at her like that, as if she really were more important to him than business.

He drew her to a halt on the path, turning her so that she had to face him. "Then what is the point, Kalinda? What are you trying to say?''

She faced him bravely. "Rand, I'm grateful for your help in this crisis. But, please, don't confuse your feelings about coming back to the business world with...with any feelings you might have for me!''

"What the hell are you talking about?" he rasped, his hands tightening forcefully around her upper arms, his face darkening.

"Please," she begged earnestly, gray eyes wide with concern for him, "don't be angry. I'm just pointing out the obvious. You're finding it exciting to get your feet wet again in the world in which you were once so successful. It was very clear yesterday that you were enjoying yourself. And if it's what you want, then I don't mind having been the catalyst that drew you out of the mountains, really I don't..."

"Catalyst!"

"Yes! Remember how I asked you a couple of

times if you were bored with your trout fishing and the little gallery? You denied it, but I think the truth is that you were getting restless. After a year and a half, you felt the urge to compete and win getting the better of you. When I came along representing a portion of the world you'd left behind, something clicked, didn't it? I became an excuse, a reason, for coming back to Denver and picking up the reins of business."

He stared at her. "You've got it all worked out, haven't you?"

"Is my conclusion so very far from the truth?" she whispered sadly. "Are you going to deny that you're enjoying yourself as you begin to wheel and deal again?"

"That's a very neat trap you've worked out, Kalinda Brady," he muttered icily, hazel eyes hardening as he surveyed her face. "I can't very well deny the fact that there is something in the business world which challenges and interests me. You saw me at work yesterday. I never stayed up half the night working on a piece of pottery!"

She nodded in mute understanding, trying to hide her unhappiness.

"And I'm not going to deny that I might have been growing bored with my lifestyle in the mountains. A year and a half of fishing and part-time employment can be a bit more than relaxing. It can make a man restless...."

"I knew it," she murmured, lowering her eyes as she listened to the confirmation of her fears.

"But you're caught in the trap with me," he went on relentlessly, lifting her chin with thumb and forefinger. "You made it very clear in a lot of little ways that you weren't interested in an affair with a lazy trout fisherman and pottery-maker! You wanted a man from your own world. Okay, you've got him. I not only understand and function very well in your world, Kalinda, I can dominate it if I wish. I'm giving you what you asked for in a man. Don't you dare try to back out of our deal now!"

Kalinda froze at the cold, hard edge in his voice. "We didn't have any sort of 'deal,' Rand!"

"We do now," he countered and crushed her lips beneath his own as if to seal it.

It was a harsh, ruthless, dominating kiss, with none of the warm, seductive persuasiveness she'd known in the past. It was as if he was intent on letting her know that he could dominate not only the world in which she made her living, but Kalinda, herself.

His mouth moved aggressively on her lips, forcing them apart and giving her no option but to accept the invasion of his tongue. Desperately Kalinda tried to pull away, break the ruthlessness of the kiss, but he only wrapped his arms around her and forced her closer. In the chill morning air he molded her body to his own, letting his inner heat trap her.

When she tried to free her lips, he used his teeth to nip warningly and she crumpled against him at the first threat. He accepted the surrender as if it were his due, not taking his mouth from hers until she had stopped fighting him completely.

When at last he lifted his head to gaze forbiddingly down at her helpless face, Kalinda sagged in his arms. He let her bury her face against his shoulder, holding her with bonds of steel.

For a long moment they stood silently. Kalinda knew she was trembling with reaction. Not just to the kiss, itself, but to all the male implacability that lay behind it. He did want her. Regardless of his other reasons for following her out of the mountains, he wanted her. Would that ever be enough?

"Don't fight me, Kalinda," he finally got out on a hoarse thread of sound. "Please don't fight me!" He turned his lips into her hair, kissing her gently now, almost apologetically. She felt a tremor go through him and knew he was shaken by the moment.

"Is that a warning, Rand?" she managed, her words muffled by the fabric of his jacket. "Are you saying I'll get hurt if I don't go along with what you want?"

His grasp on her tautened. "I would never hurt

you, honey. But I can't let you go, either. I need you too much!''

"Rand..."

She wasn't sure just what she was going to say under the tension of the moment, but whatever it might have been died in her throat as he gently set her a little ways from him and forced a quirking smile.

"Don't say anything more this morning, sweetheart. For both our sakes, I think we'd better get back to business. Come on, let's go find ourselves some breakfast.''

Without waiting for a response, he tugged her gently down the path.

The rest of the day passed much as the preceding one. Rand was constantly on the phone to banks, old acquaintances who owed him favors, and people who knew an astonishing amount about the inside workings of David Hutton's fledgling empire. When he wasn't using her telephone, he was going through the endless paperwork generated by a thriving enterprise such as Brady Data Processing.

"You know, this whole thing is turning out to be quite an education," Kalinda observed truthfully at one point as they munched sandwiches and prepared once more to stay late at the office. "I'm going to be a much more aware businesswoman when this is all over!"

He smiled, a genuine flash of humor. "That's one

thing that can be said about a company that gets caught up in a merger battle. Management is never quite the same thereafter.''

"A matter of facing reality, I suppose," she nodded seriously.

He took her home that night around ten o'clock and he didn't try to invite himself inside. Kalinda thought he looked rather preoccupied, in fact, and wondered at his almost casual good-night kiss. But she didn't argue with it. She knew she needed the time to herself.

But she came to no revealing conclusions as she lay alone in her bed. Instead, she found herself dreaming that Rand was beside her. When she went into work the next morning, she didn't try to deny her own eagerness to see him again.

He was there ahead of her, already on his second cup of coffee apparently and he looked up inquiringly as she stood in her doorway.

"I give up," he smiled. "Why the frown?"

"You're drinking too much coffee," she said with automatic concern as she walked into the room and seated herself behind the mahogany desk.

He glanced down at his cup in surprise. "An old habit, I guess."

"A little caffeine goes a long way. I think you should switch to tea."

He studied her determined expression for a long

moment and then pushed aside his half-finished cup. "Whatever you say, boss."

That made her grin. "There's nothing quite like a truly deferential, obedient employee!"

"I'll make a bargain with you. I'll be deferential and obedient on the job if you'll be deferential and obedient after hours!"

"Facetiousness and flippancy in employees, however, is not condoned in the offices of Brady Data Processing!"

"I'll try to remember that. Now, suppose you pour me a cup of tea?" he suggested smoothly, eyes gleaming.

She thought about that. "If I do you're liable to get the notion you can manipulate the boss."

"The only time I intend to manipulate the boss is in bed," he growled, leaning forward with just enough menace to make her sit back in her chair.

"You *have* been up in those mountains too long," Kalinda complained, jumping to her feet and striding quickly over to where a pot of hot water simmered on a hot plate alongside a pot of coffee. "You've forgotten your office manners!"

"I'll rely on you to keep me in line," he chuckled as she returned with a mug of tea. He accepted it with a smile but there was something in his eyes that told her he'd meant what he just said. He'd rely on her to keep him in line? That didn't make any sense.

"What's the battle plan for today?" she questioned in a decidedly business voice, eyeing him pointedly.

"Today we plan dinner," he announced, sipping the hot tea and watching her interestedly over the rim.

"Dinner!"

"Dinner at the restaurant where David Hutton will be dining tonight," he amended casually.

She stared at him. "But why?"

"Financial maneuvering is only half this battle," he explained calmly. "Psychology is a critical aspect, too."

"You want him to see you out with me?" she hazarded as his line of reasoning clicked in her brain.

"By now he knows I'm involved with Brady. Tonight he'll find out just how much."

"But why?"

"So he'll see that there's no point in trying to subvert me," Rand told her carelessly.

"Subvert you! Good lord! Rand, are you telling me he might try buying you off?"

"He already has. I got the call last night after I'd taken you home." Rand appeared totally unconcerned. "It's a logical step. I didn't talk to Hutton directly, of course, I just received a feeler from one of his high-ranking employees."

"My God!" Kalinda shook her head, unable to

believe it. "What...what did you tell the person who called you?" Somehow she had never envisioned such a ploy on Hutton's part. She knew such tactics were used but they had never impinged on her world. Kalinda found herself wondering for the first time if sharks could be bribed.

"What do you think I said?" Rand muttered gruffly.

She stared at him, assessing, remembering, analyzing and finally came up with the only possible conclusion. "You told him no, of course."

"Why 'of course'?" he demanded interestedly, watching her intently.

"You would never break your word to us," she replied positively, relaxing slightly as she realized it was the simple truth.

There was a tension-filled moment as they sat regarding each other in silent understanding and then Rand smiled gently.

"Thank you, Kalinda."

She shrugged. She trusted him. There was nothing more to say on that subject. "So why are we having dinner in the same restaurant tonight?"

"Because he'll try upping the offer again and again, thinking he only has to find the right price. I want to squash that notion flat. I want to start closing doors on him as rapidly and as solidly as possible so that he begins to panic." Rand spoke intently, a frown of concentration creasing his forehead. "If we can turn the tables on him quickly enough, I think we can get him to withdraw the offer. He has to know we've got a whole series of options and we'll use every damn one of them until he's out in the cold."

"Have we really got a whole series of options?"

"Yes, but most of them are expensive. It would be nice if we can kill his interest before we have to resort to them."

"What's the worst possible case?" Kalinda asked bluntly.

"A friendly merger with another company," he told her, not shielding the truth.

She groaned. "I was afraid of that. A white knight?"

He nodded, tossing down the stack of papers he had been reading. "That's what the 'friendly' company is usually called in cases like this. It can be done, Kalinda. I have contacts. We can find a friendly suitor for Brady Data Processing who will agree to merge with us on our terms. It's better than turning everything over to Hutton!"

"I know. But even in the friendliest of situations, Brady Data Processing will lose some of its autonomy."

"If it comes to that, we'll negotiate very carefully. But there's another option, I think. You have surprisingly good credit for a company this size. Your assets are solid and generally rather understated. I think, with a little fast talking, we might be able to get that line of credit expanded.''

''For what purpose?''

''So that Brady can better Hutton's offer for its own shares,'' he said quietly.

''A tender offer for our own shares? That would be expensive,'' she whispered thoughtfully. ''Credit costs a fortune these days. Interest rates are high....''

''I notice from your records that you've been shy of using bank credit in the past, Kalinda.''

''I have an instinctive dislike of being in debt, I suppose,'' she admitted dryly. ''A holdover from Dad.''

''But borrowed money is the way big businesses are run these days. Brady is going to have to recognize that if it wants to stay competitive and autonomous.'' Rand spread out a financial report and began talking in detail.

Kalinda listened, fascinated with the expertise she was witnessing. Where would Rand Alastair have been today if he hadn't dropped out a year and a half ago? The thought crossed her mind that he might be the one trying to take over Brady Data Processing. She wouldn't have stood a chance!

Properly appreciative of the importance of fighting David Hutton on all levels, Kalinda dressed with care for the important evening. She chose a dinner suit of rich, printed velvet. The small, shaped jacket fit over a softer velvet skirt and a silk blouse complimented the chic combination. Over it she flung a dashing sequined and fringed shawl. Hair sleek and held with a glittering comb, she looked sophisticated and elegantly sure of herself. Which was exactly the note she wanted to set in front of David, she told herself.

As she dressed she thought again of how close she had come to confronting him in the little mountain town. Even if Rand Alastair failed to save Brady Data Processing, she would always be grateful for his having to put a stop to the ill-advised attempt at revenge. She didn't even want to think of all the disastrous complications that might have ensued. Somehow, she knew, David would have used the confrontation against her, perhaps to compromise her in front of her own staff. There was no doubt about it, she'd had a close call. What if Hutton had gotten word to Brady management that the company's president was secretly meeting its biggest enemy?

Her gray eyes were sparkling with inner excitement when she opened the door to Rand that evening. And as she took in the sight of him in a hand-tailored evening jacket and dark trousers, she acknowledged that the excitement she was feeling wasn't just for the adventure of combating David Hutton.

"We both look dressed to kill this evening, don't we?" she laughed as they stood admiring each other.

"Very appropriate," he murmured, taking her arm. "That's exactly what we're going to try to accomplish. A little killing."

"How did you know where David would be dining tonight?" she remembered to ask fifteen minutes later as Rand turned the Lotus over to a valet parking attendant and started her toward the expensive restaurant.

"I'm afraid I made use of your secretary," he admitted.

"George?"

"I can see why you hired him. George is a very competent person. He managed to get the information out of Hutton's secretary without even giving her a clue about what was going on behind the scenes."

Kalinda had a mental image of George smoothly extracting the information he wanted and grinned. She was still smiling as they were shown graciously to an intimate table for two.

Rand saw Kalinda idly taking in the candlelit scene of white linen, shining silver and fresh flowers and grimaced.

"Please don't tell me Hutton used to bring you here a lot," he ordered gruffly, reaching for the wine list.

"He didn't. The place wasn't open back then," she smiled obligingly. She thought fleetingly of the whirlwind courtship David had given her and realized with a start that the memory no longer had any power. She felt neither the flash of anger or the hurt she'd once known.

"Good," he stated evenly. "I wouldn't want any misty memories coming forth to mar the image we're trying to establish tonight!"

"There aren't any," she replied easily, smiling at him across the flickering flame of the candle. She met his eyes with total honesty and he nodded, apparently satisfied.

"But I could use a little guidance on how to play the coming scene," she went on determinedly. "Are we supposed to create the impression of boss and consultant holding a dinner conference? Or should I let him think you're an old friend of the family who stepped in to give me a hand because of a friendship you once had with Dad? Or…"

"I never met your father," he reminded her with an enigmatic smile.

"But it would lend a nice touch to the 'image', wouldn't it?" she suggested seriously, struck with the brilliance of her own idea.

"Just follow my lead, all right?" he said repressively.

"But what, exactly, is your lead?"

"You'll see… Ah! Here he comes now. Looks just like his picture."

Kalinda stiffened, the sense of adventure going out of the evening as reality intruded. She looked at Rand, watching for some sort of signal, some indication of how to greet David.

And then the other couple was beside the table and Rand was getting politely to his feet as David came to a pointed halt.

"Good evening, Kalinda," the well-remembered voice said suavely. "I hadn't expected to see you here tonight. I don't believe you ever met my wife. Darling, this is Kalinda Brady. She and I are presently involved in some business negotiations."

Kalinda could have screamed at the harmless way in which he said that, but she looked beyond David's handsome features to the face of the woman she had used as one of the arguments for not going through with the confrontation with David.

It was a lovely, charming face, a face that said the other woman knew nothing about the darker side of her husband's nature and preferred it that way.

"Good evening, Mrs. Hutton," Kalinda said politely, holding out her hand. It was taken graciously as the other woman smiled and said something polite in return. And then Kalinda glanced at Rand, preparing to introduce him.

"I don't believe we've met," Rand was already saying smoothly, before Kalinda could get the proper words out of her mouth. He looked straight at David. "I'm Rand Alastair, Kalinda's fiancé."

Nine

Only David Hutton's wife appeared to accept Rand's deceptively casual announcement at face value. Kalinda decided rather cynically that she and David both owed Mrs. Hutton a vote of thanks for giving them time to recover from the shock.

With polished charm the lovely woman at David's side extended her congratulations and made the proper remarks. Rand responded to her calmly, easily, until they were interrupted by David who had obviously managed to begin reasoning things out.

"I hadn't realized you were engaged, Kalinda." The dark gaze that Kalinda had once found so attractive pierced her, looking for the lie.

"It's a very recent development," she explained, astonished at her own coolness. She flicked a quick look at Rand who came to her rescue.

"Last weekend, in fact," he elaborated, smiling fondly at Kalinda who felt herself redden. "We haven't even had a chance to buy a ring. We were on vacation in the mountains," he went on, speaking apparently to David's wife. "Soon after we arrived back in town we discovered some rather urgent business had developed."

Kalinda felt David stiffen at the words, his narrow gaze going to Rand's hard profile.

"Kalinda and I will have to settle the business matters this week and then we'll have time for all the little niceties of an engagement." Rand turned his head with an amused gleam in his hazel eyes, catching David Hutton's assessing glance. "Nothing very complicated, so it shouldn't take too long."

"I had heard you'd gone to work for Brady Data Processing," David said coldly. "It must have taken the promise of a considerable financial reward to draw you out of retirement...."

"Money, I'm afraid, had nothing to do with it. Kalinda was the reason I decided to get involved in the business world again."

Kalinda felt a happy warmth flood her veins. Rand had just made it very clear his interest in going to war against David was entirely personal, not monetary. He could not be bought.

"I see," David said icily. "You don't appear to think this rather urgent business matter you mentioned will take long to settle?"

"Not at all." Rand smiled his shark's smile. "A quite simple bit of corporate game-playing. I've had a great deal of experience in this sort of thing, as you may know. In this instance, it's all a piece of cake. Kalinda's firm is surprisingly strong. Her credit flexibility would astound you. I rather think when the current matter is settled I may encourage her to do a little corporate hunting. Brady is in a very strong position to get involved with the merger craze as a buyer."

The meaning in his words hung in the air, unsaid, but clear. Brady Data Processing might soon be seriously looking at David Hutton's firm as a potential acquisition. The thought of turning the tables on David nearly made Kalinda laugh. It was all she could do to maintain only a polite, amused smile.

"That's enough business for tonight, David," Hutton's wife was saying cheerfully, a fine-boned hand on her husband's sleeve. "We really should leave these two by themselves. They're probably taking an evening to celebrate their engagement…?"

"How did you guess?" Rand said dryly.

"Yes, of course, my dear," David said absently, his angry gaze on Kalinda's amused expression.

Her smile broadened as she politely inclined her head in farewell. There was so much David wanted to say and so little he could say under the circumstances. She saw it all in those handsome dark eyes. He was calling her every name in the book, frustrated, angry, and beginning to perceive his own potential failure.

Without a word he turned and walked stiffly away with his wife. Rand sat down slowly, his thoughtful gaze on his opponent.

Kalinda didn't hesitate. Leaning forward, she hissed, "You might have warned me!"

"It was a spur-of-the-moment inspiration," he defended, his gaze swiveling back to her accusing features.

"The hell it was! You've been planning this all day. Why didn't you tell me you were going to let David think we were engaged?"

"Because I thought I'd only get a lot of static from you," he retorted imperturbably, reaching once more for the wine menu as the wine steward approached.

Kalinda sat impatiently, one toe tapping the carpet in irritation as Rand deliberated with the steward. When they were alone again she resumed the attack.

"Aren't you afraid you might talk yourself into

a corner with lies like that one?'' she grumbled, wishing with all her heart it hadn't been a lie; that Rand wanted to marry her, not just have an affair.

"I have never talked myself into a corner I didn't want to be in or couldn't get out of if I wished,'' he declared emphatically, beginning to study the list of delicate salads on the front page of the menu.

"Well, that's very nice for you, but what about me?'' she protested feelingly, annoyed at his casual arrogance. "Word of this so-called engagement is going to go around like wildfire. I have no desire to go through the process of being jilted again! It's...it's humiliating!''

Even as she spoke, Kalinda thought ahead to just what Rand's announcement might mean. It was easy for him to use whatever tactics came to hand in this business battle, but she was the one who was going to be left to deal with the aftermath. And right now the aftermath of an affair seemed far more depressing than the aftermath of a merger action.

Rand set his menu down with care, eyes turning a little golden in the flickering candlelight as he caught her half-accusing, half-despairing look.

"Do you really believe I would deliberately humiliate you, Kalinda?'' he asked softly.

The simple question stopped her in her tracks, effectively cutting off the flow of angry words she had been preparing to launch as the full realization of her new predicament registered. It struck her very forcibly that this was the second time that day Rand had asked her for a show of faith. The first had occurred that morning when he'd asked her if she thought he'd let Hutton buy him off.

She eyed him thoughtfully, wondering why he was pinning her down like this. But forced to consider the question in depth, rather than in irritation, she knew there could be only one answer.

"No," she sighed, sitting back in her chair and lifting her chin with a regal air. "I don't believe you would deliberately humiliate me, Rand."

There was a long, weighty pause while the implications of her confession hovered between them. Rand's eyes never left hers and she could have sworn there was the faintest of smiles playing at the edge of his mouth.

"So why," Kalinda went on steadily, needing to know the answer, "did you use that line on David?"

"Number one because it was effective...."

Kalinda said nothing, waiting for number two.

"And number two," he went on obligingly, "because I think the idea has a lot of intrinsic merit."

"Meaning?" she challenged bravely.

"You and I make a good team, Kalinda," he began intently. "We work well together, we're attracted to each other, we're..."

"Is this a proposal?" she gasped, horrified.

"If you like…"

"If I like! I have never heard such an unromantic, unemotional suggestion in my life! You might as well be proposing a…a *merger!*" Kalinda felt like crying and heaving the crystal at him at the same time. How dare he sit there and calmly suggest a business arrangement?

"A *friendly* merger," he emphasized dryly, his eyes wary.

"Not so long ago you only wanted an affair!" she reminded him tightly.

"There are other factors involved now, don't you think?" he asked reasonably.

"Business factors!"

"May I take it from your seething expression that you're turning down my proposal?" he inquired politely, his eyes enigmatic.

"You may consider the proposal hurled back in your teeth!"

"Then I'm off the hook? There will be no future accusations that I've deliberately humiliated you?" he drawled.

She whitened, shocked by the twist in the argument. Desperately she grabbed at her pride and her strength of will. "You…you may consider yourself quite free," she muttered. "You have, after all, given me my chance, haven't you?"

He shrugged. "It wouldn't have been a bad arrangement, Kalinda."

"No wonder you call yourself a shark when it comes to business. You can be quite cold-blooded, can't you?" she snapped, desperately using anger to shore up her willpower. She was deeply shocked at her desire to say yes to his proposal; to accept him on any terms.

Something in him hardened perceptibly. "I would think that 'cold-blooded' is the one accusation you wouldn't make. You are, after all, in a position to judge the issue. Have I ever been cold toward you, Kalinda?"

She ground her teeth. "That's got nothing to do with this!"

Suddenly a slow grin began to replace the firmly marked line of his lips and the hazel eyes softened. "Does it strike you that you're on the verge of becoming slightly irrational in your arguments? It's a good sign, actually. It gives me hope."

Kalinda's hands knotted the white linen napkin in her lap but her voice was properly flippant. "A good businessman doesn't rely on hope. He relies on facts and figures."

"You're wrong, you know. Business people are essentially optimists. Who else but an optimist would wager such vast sums of money on anything as tricky as competing in the national economic marketplace?"

"Are you going to argue with me all evening?"

"No, honey, I'm not. I'm going to enjoy this

evening and I'm going to do my damnedest to see that you enjoy it, too!''

"Of course. We have an image to maintain, don't we? As long as David and his wife are in the vicinity…''

"We shall do our best to appear the happily engaged couple," he concluded firmly.

And much to Kalinda's surprise, Rand proceeded to do exactly that. He was charming and attentive. He entertained her throughout the first course until she finally began to relax and respond to the intelligent, amusing conversation.

By the time the entrée arrived, she had firmly pushed the depressing business proposal into the background of her mind, telling herself that it had all arisen out of Rand's determination to help her defend Brady Data Processing. It wasn't his fault she had overreacted.

They were lingering over dessert, a fresh raspberry torte, when Kalinda glanced up to see David and his wife leaving. The other couple did not stop to say good-night to Rand and Kalinda.

"Are you beginning to find it amusing?" Rand inquired blandly.

"David's reaction to us? Yes, I am. I could almost see the little wheels going around in his head when he realized you were firmly on the side of Brady," she admitted, grinning.

"So I'm forgiven for my claim to being your fiancé?" he asked whimsically.

"I'm sorry I blew up," she apologized meekly. "It's just that it took me by surprise. You should have warned me, Rand."

"I was afraid you wouldn't agree to it."

"So you sprung it on me just as you sprung it on David." She shook her head. "When I first met you in the mountains I kept telling myself your talents were being wasted. I was right."

"I'm not sure that's a compliment," he groaned. "But I'll let it go for now. Are you finished?"

"One last raspberry."

"Good. It's a shame to waste all these fine feathers we're wearing. I thought we'd go dancing at a nightclub I used to know near here."

Kalinda made no protest, knowing in her heart that she would do anything to prolong the evening. Anything to prolong her fragile, dangerous relationship with Rand Alastair.

A few moments later, the fringed, sequined stole glittering around her shoulders, Kalinda found herself gently stuffed into the front seat of the Lotus. When Rand slid in beside her, turning to smile, she became very aware of the dark intimacy of the small car. And of the proposal she had just turned down.

There was little conversation between them as Rand drove to the nightclub, a delicate, stirring, undeniably sensual feeling permeating the confined atmosphere. Kalinda didn't want to fight it even though she knew she should.

But the evening had made her realize how tenuous her relationship with Rand now was. He would help her stave off David Hutton's takeover bid, but after that there would be nothing to keep him by her side. She sensed he still desired her, but she couldn't shake the feeling his need was somehow connected with the fact that she had been his ticket back to the business world. He claimed he'd come back to prove himself to her, but she was far too aware of the satisfaction he was taking in the effort. Rand had wanted an excuse to come back to the thing he knew best and she had been that excuse.

Torn by the knowledge that she would have leaped at his proposal if it had been delivered with even a modicum of love, Kalinda sought to justify her response when Rand took her into his arms on the dance floor. If she wasn't going to marry the man, why was she clinging to him like this? There was no future, or at least not one which boded well. Why prolong the agony of a final good-bye?

His arms slid warmly around her waist as the soft, slow music drifted through the dark, romantic nightclub. Other couples moved nearby, each lost in a private world. Kalinda rested her head on

Rand's shoulder, her arms moving with an aching intimacy around his neck.

Rand's fingers gently kneaded the curve of her hip as he pulled her close. "I think we make a very convincing engaged couple," he murmured in her hair. "No, don't you dare tense up on me. I was merely stating a fact. Did you forget how good we are together when you turned down my proposal this evening?"

"Mutual desire is not enough to justify marriage," she whispered into the fabric of his jacket.

"But it is enough to justify an affair, isn't it?" he whispered deeply, lips grazing the top of her ear. He pressed her closer, deliberately melding her body with his until she was keenly aware of the hard warmth and the beginnings of arousal in him.

"Rand, I don't think we ought..."

Her fumbling words were gently cut off as he turned her head with one hand and kissed her. It was an incredibly seductive experience, Kalinda discovered, to be kissed on a dance floor. The lazy, probing passion of it somehow combined with the flow of music and the gleaming shadows. She melted against him as she always seemed to do when he held her like this.

Sensing her surrender to the moment, Rand slowly, deliberately began to increase the physical tension already blossoming between them. His mouth moved moistly on hers, parting her lips, sipping her honey. He used his hands to fit her close to the cradle of his thighs, shifting his feet occasionally so that his leg somehow lodged suggestively between hers.

Kalinda knew the need and want in her was being coaxed into a smoldering fire but she told herself she was safe enough on the dance floor. And when he took her home later she would have the long ride in the Lotus during which to cool off.

He lifted his mouth from hers, finding the nape of her neck, the line of her jaw, the edge of her eyebrow with his lips. Kalinda shivered and she could feel his satisfaction at the obvious sign of her response.

"Why did you turn down my proposal tonight, sweetheart?" he asked gently.

"I came much too close to a...a business marriage once before," she breathed shakily, not meeting his eyes. She wished he would stop talking and just hold her.

"And you're afraid that's all it would be between us?" he pressed huskily.

"I think Brady Data Processing is only a first step for you on your road back to an empire. I don't want to be used...."

"Used!"

"I know you wouldn't do it deliberately," she placated urgently, feathering her fingertips on the back of his neck. "You really believe you're offering a fair deal."

"Aren't I?" he demanded roughly.

"I suppose. But it's not enough…" she trailed off helplessly at the glittering expression in his gaze.

"Then that leaves us with the affair, doesn't it?" he said coldly.

She drew in her breath, knowing the seductive moment was over and she now had to make her stand. The same stand she had tried to make during the early-morning walk in the park.

"I don't think that's very wise, Rand," she began steadily. "You need time to readjust to the business world. Your interest in me is bound to be fleeting once you've reestablished yourself."

"And you're afraid I'd be using you, just as you're afraid I'd be using you if we were to marry," he broke in grimly.

"Wouldn't you?" she dared, lifting her lashes to meet his eyes.

"Use you? I don't care what you call it at this point," he bit out with impatient savagery. "Whatever it is, it's going to happen. Because I'm going to take you back to your apartment tonight and make love to you until you are no longer capable of finding reasons for it *not* to happen!"

"Rand!" His name was almost a cry. He meant it. She could see the intention in his eyes, knew he wouldn't be stopped now that he'd made up his mind.

"Come on, Kalinda," he ordered, his tone softening but becoming no less determined. "Let's go home."

The tension that tautened between them on the drive back to Kalinda's town house was palpable. It was also very silent. Kalinda didn't know what Rand was thinking, but she knew her own mind was whirling with arguments and counter-arguments. He intended to make love to her tonight and she knew of no practical way of stopping him because, deep down, it was what she wanted, too.

Rand said nothing as he guided her forcefully through the door of her home and locked it firmly behind them. And he said nothing as she tried to step nervously out of reach.

But his hand closed on her upper arm in an unshakable grip and she was hauled against his chest, the sequined shawl slipping unnoticed to the green carpet to lie in a sparkling heap.

Wordlessly they stared at each other and then whatever bits of protest Kalinda might have found were blocked as Rand began to renew the claim he had on her.

She should have known, Kalinda told herself as he rained aggressive, mastering kisses down her throat, that she could never withstand such a sensuous assault. The need in him was genuine even though at this moment it was combined with a desire to subdue. And her desire to match and satisfy that need was equally genuine, even though she told herself it was a dangerous path. She couldn't fight her own love for him.

"Kalinda, you can't deny this feeling between us. You can't possibly say it's based on business!" The words were grated roughly against her skin as he began to undo the velvet jacket.

"No, Rand," she acknowledged gently as the jacket fell to the floor beside the sequined shawl.

"Admit you want me, sweetheart," he commanded gruffly, sliding the silk blouse off her shoulders. "You must know I want you. Admit that you feel the same. Neither of us could walk away from an affair!"

It was the simple truth. With a moan of acceptance of her fate, Kalinda wound her arms around his neck, returning his kisses with passionate, yielding intensity. She had no choice but to acknowledge the effect he had on her and to admit her inability to walk away from him. He might not know it was based on love, but she knew it.

"I want you, Rand," she whispered against his throat as his hands found her breasts and began bringing them to fullness. She wanted to say she loved him but knew he wouldn't want her love. He wanted an affair and, perhaps, a business-oriented marriage.

"I know that, darling," he husked. "You can't hide it. I see it every time I look in your eyes, every time your body comes alive under my hands. But it's so damn frustrating hearing you try to wriggle out of our affair!"

"I won't try anymore," she vowed thickly, pushing his dinner jacket onto the floor with inviting, eager hands. She went to work on the buttons of his shirt. "I should have known I couldn't out-reason a skilled manipulator like you," she added wistfully, her mouth lifting at the corners.

"Not when you're all wrong in your reasoning process!"

"Am I, Rand?" she whispered.

"Yes," he growled as the last of their clothes fell to the carpet. "All wrong…"

He ran his hands caressingly down her back, sinking his fingers into the curve of her bottom and letting her feel the hardening maleness of him against her thighs.

Kalinda spread her fingers across his chest, delighting in the roughness of the crisp hair even as his hair-roughened leg moved boldly between hers.

She closed her eyes in expectation as he bent to lift her into his arms. But instead of carrying her into the bedroom, he settled her on the thick green carpet beside the pile of clothes.

He came down beside her, sweeping his hand across her breasts, pausing to draw teasing circles around each nipple before moving lower. She turned into his arms, the need in her shining in her eyes.

"Did you really think I'd let you try to talk me out of an affair?" he demanded hoarsely, pinning her gently to the carpet with his leg.

"Yes, no, I don't know. I haven't been thinking all that clearly lately." She reached up and pulled his head down to hers.

Committed now, she kissed him with all the longing in her heart, using the ancient, womanly wiles buried in every nerve ending. Letting her own need and desire take over she explored his mouth with a passion that clearly aroused him deeply. Once more, as she always seemed to do with this man, Kalinda put the future aside. It just didn't seem as important as expressing her love in the present. Even if that love must remain mute.

She felt his fingers on her thighs and then released his head as he groaned and began to kiss her breasts. Fingers locked in his chestnut hair, she held him to her and let her senses swirl.

"You're so perfect for me," he said throatily. "So exactly what I need. You must see I can't give you up, sweetheart."

She arched upward and felt his lips on her thigh. The tiny, stinging caress nearly drove her insane with desire. The shimmering, promising currents began gathering once again in her body, seeking the release they had learned to expect from this man.

He caught her arching hips with his hand, holding her in delicious bondage as she struggled to complete the union. The sensation of being held back seemed to hone her need to an even higher peak. Kalinda twisted and curled, grateful for each new teasing, tormenting touch, but determined to have it all.

"Please, Rand, please," she begged, grasping at him, trying to pull him down on top of her.

He kissed her navel and then the slope of her small breasts, letting her writhe against him but not letting her take control of the lovemaking.

"Tell me again that you want me, sweetheart," he whispered beguilingly.

"I want you. Oh, God! How I want you!" Trapped in the depths of her own desire she would have told him the truth if he had asked it of her. She would have willingly told him of her love. But he didn't ask that question. Instead, incredibly, he asked another. One she wasn't prepared for at all.

"If you really want me so much," he grated heavily, "then there's no reason for us not to marry, is there? I could never tolerate letting you go to another man after what we've shared. Say you'll marry me, sweet Kalinda. Make the engagement real."

Stunned by the demand, Kalinda tried to think logically, tried to remember her fears. But it was impossible to do so while cradled so tightly against him. She loved him and he was asking her to marry him.

Weakened with longing and unable to argue with herself in that moment, Kalinda heard herself whisper the answer.

"Yes, Rand. I'll marry you. I'll do anything you want."

Nothing had changed. She knew the odds were that he was still caught up in a combination of desire and gratitude to her for providing him the excuse he'd needed to return to the business world. He had said nothing of love.

But she no longer had the strength to turn down that which her heart so desperately wanted. She loved him. Perhaps, in time, she could teach him to love her. If not, if the time ever came when he realized he no longer needed her, she would not regret the time she'd been his. Real love might eventually cause sadness, but not regret.

Ten

Two days later a somewhat tired-looking Rand appeared in Kalinda's office doorway. She had seen him only at work since the night he had seduced her into marrying him. He'd made compelling love to her on the plush carpet, whispering words of aching need. And when it was over he'd carried her tenderly to the bedroom, kissed her good-night, dressed, and left.

The next day at work he had been all business, never mentioning the traumatic events of the evening. He had devoted himself to his task at Brady with single-minded determination. She knew he'd talked to people high up in David Hutton's firm, spelling out exactly how Brady Data Processing was prepared to match the hostile merger offer to shareholders or to find a friendly corporate marriage partner. That night he'd taken Kalinda home late after work and left her politely on her doorstep.

She had just put down the receiver, a small smile on her face as she considered David Hutton's call when Rand appeared, leaning in the doorway with deceptive casualness. But she saw the flicker of excitement and satisfaction in his eyes.

"It's all over but the shouting, honey," he advised laconically. "You should be hearing something soon. I just talked to my contact at Hutton's firm. They're throwing in the towel. We're...I mean, you're going to get out of this relatively unscathed."

"Thanks to you." Her smile broadened as she absorbed the manner in which he was hiding his personal satisfaction. "I just got word from David, himself." She gestured at the telephone.

Rand lifted one chestnut brow inquiringly. "So soon?"

"He's withdrawing the offer." She decided there was no point mentioning what David had said prior to calling off the hostile merger attempt. "He wasn't particularly pleased, but you managed to leave him with very little option. He can't afford us. Not with the kind of credit we can command at the banks."

"He was counting on Brady's traditional dislike

of using credit," Rand nodded as if to himself. "And sheer panic."

"Which didn't develop because we knew we had the best player on our team," Kalinda inserted warmly. There was something more than satisfaction in Rand's expression. A hint of anxiety? Perhaps even wariness? She didn't understand it, but if it was simply a matter of his ego needing a little stroking she had no objections. He deserved it.

"It's over, Rand, and you're the reason Brady is still an independent concern," Kalinda depressed the intercom button and leaned forward slightly. "George, would you please round everyone up in the main conference room as soon as possible?"

"Everyone, Miss Brady, or just management?" George asked carefully. He knew she'd just taken a call from David Hutton.

"Everyone, George. Including you."

There was a fractional hesitation and then George's curiosity got the better of him. "Good news, Miss Brady? Or bad?"

"The best, George. And as soon as you notify everyone about the meeting would you mind taking a minute to find us a place that can accommodate a celebration this afternoon?"

"A place that will accommodate *everyone?*" he stressed cautiously.

"The entire staff, George."

"Yes, Miss Brady."

She released the intercom button and stood up, meeting Rand's dryly amused gaze.

"What's the matter?" she grinned. "Not used to being on the side of the underdog?"

He winced, as if she'd stung him. "Frankly, I've never seen it from this side," he admitted.

"Well, I'll have to confess this is the first time we at Brady have had this particular excuse for celebrating. But we've had practice at the annual Christmas party!" She spoke lightly, trying to erase whatever it was she'd just said that had made him look so rueful.

"You'll be picking up the tab personally?" Rand asked.

"We don't run to office slush funds here at Brady," she affirmed with a grimace. "I'll be paying the bill. But it will be worth it."

Two hours later the jubilant Brady staff adjourned from work early to take an extended lunch hour which, Kalinda guessed with amusement, would last all afternoon.

George had succeeded in finding a colorful beer and pizza tavern that was willing to welcome so many people on such short notice. Foaming mugs of beer and pizzas with "everything" were being ordered unstintingly. Kalinda decided not to concern herself with the inevitable price tag. It was far cheaper than a merger would have been!

She glanced around the room as the staff began

to break up into familiar groups. George sat at a corner table surrounded by the other secretaries, all female. The word processing group had claimed another table nearby. First-line supervisors were drifting cheerfully into their own territory and Brady's upper management occupied a long table with Kalinda and Rand in the center.

Kalinda smothered a grin as a toast went up, beer mugs on high. It was one of several and the subject this time was Rand. She could have sworn he was turning a dull red. Amused, she leaned close and under cover of the cheers, whispered, "One thing about being on the side of the good guys: We're big on heroes!"

In the dim light, Kalinda was positive Rand turned an even darker shade of red as he slanted her a wry glance.

"It's not a role I'm accustomed to playing."

"Hero? But you're a natural for the part!"

He looked at her with sudden sharpness. "You think so?"

"Definitely," she laughed.

He continued looking at her levelly for a long moment. "Kalinda, I have to talk to you."

"Now?"

"As soon as possible."

She chilled, remembering the wariness in him earlier. What was wrong? Had he changed his mind about the marriage already? Realized he was now back in his natural milieu and no longer needed her? Beneath the rustically carved table, Kalinda's palms went strangely damp.

"All right, Rand. I don't think we'll be missed." She didn't look at him as she spoke.

There were several good-natured calls protesting their departure, but no one seemed unduly upset. In fact, Kalinda thought sardonically, everyone looked a little too understanding; a little too smugly pleased. It didn't take much insight to realize her slightly feudal staff had decided Rand would make an excellent consort for their president!

Rand drove back to his apartment without speaking, the white-knuckled grip of his hands on the wheel the chief evidence of the intensity of his thoughts. It made Kalinda even more nervous.

Perhaps…perhaps he would go back to the idea of continuing the affair. She could live without marriage, but she didn't even want to consider living without him altogether. Rand had bound them together on too many levels, made her too much a part of him. She would never be free again.

Kalinda's tension drove her to precipitate the confrontation. She must know what was happening. As soon as he opened the door of the apartment she stepped inside and turned proudly to face him.

"What is it, Rand? What's wrong?"

He shut the door and leaned back against it, his hands on the knob as if he needed to brace himself.

There was hard determination in every line of his body.

"Kalinda, I've done a lot of thinking since the night you agreed to marry me."

"Have you?" What could she say? How could she stop him?

"I had to finish what I started at Brady. I had to stop Hutton's takeover...."

She waited, not understanding.

His mouth hardened. "I realize that in so doing, in showing you I could operate effectively in your world, I've complicated matters between us."

"How?" It was almost a plea.

"It's obvious," he said grimly. "I've made you afraid of me."

He stepped away from the door, lifting a hand to stop the impulsive denial which leaped to her lips. "No, it's true. I wanted you to be proud of me, to admire me. And instead, I've given you every reason to fear me. That's why you tried to call off the affair, isn't it? Why I had to trick and seduce you into agreeing to marry me. My brilliant plan has backfired. I realized that after I left you the other night. And I've seen the wariness in you for the past couple of days."

"But, Rand...!"

He shook his head, walking restlessly to stare out the window. "I honestly don't know how to reassure you, except with time. I thought about putting off the marriage, but I can't bring myself to make the sacrifice. Selfish, I know, but ask anyone: Selfishness is one of my prime character traits.''

"Rand," Kalinda broke in a little breathlessly, hope and despair shredding her nerves. "What is it you think I'm afraid of?"

"That I'll take Brady away from you. Use it as the foundation of a new conglomerate controlled by me. In short, that I'll do to you what Hutton tried to do two years ago and again this week," he told her flatly, keeping his back to her.

She stared at the sleek, proud head, her heart almost too full for words.

"You idiot," she managed lovingly. "That thought never entered my mind."

The broad shoulders were held tautly. "You thought I was using you…"

"Not in that sense. I was only afraid that you were using me in your own mind as an excuse for coming back to Denver and your old life. I didn't want you confusing your emotions for me with those for your work. I certainly never thought you'd try to take Brady from me! Ask David Hutton," she concluded bluntly as he swung around almost violently.

"Hutton!"

"Oh, yes," she smiled, remembering the phone call that morning. "It was his last-ditch effort. He tried to tell me what you would do to me and the firm once you had salvaged it from his grasp. Tried to convince me I was much better off turning everything over to him.''

''What did you tell him?'' The question was low-voiced and vulnerable.

''The same thing I'm going to tell you. I trust you completely, Rand.'' She didn't move, but she knew her eyes would be reflecting her love and trust.

He watched her with a hunger that had nothing to do with physical desire.

''Do you realize,'' he said, each word deliberate and carved with dazed wonder, ''you're probably the only human being in the Rocky Mountain Empire who has ever said that to me?'' He came forward, pulling her into his arms as if he were afraid she might break.

''Oh, my darling Kalinda, that's one of the reasons I need you so much. I need someone who believes in me. I know you haven't had time to fall in love with me but you want me, you can't hide that, and you trust me. Surely that's a start. Someday I'll make you love me as much as I love you. I swear it!''

Kalinda felt him tremble as she pressed her face into his shoulder. ''And to think,'' she whispered shakily, ''that I once credited you with an unusual degree of perception!''

''What's that supposed to mean?'' he demanded.

"I love you, Rand. From the beginning, I think. I knew when I left you that morning in the mountains I'd never be completely free of you. I knew I'd never fully recover from my 'vacation fling.' When you showed up at my door the night of the party I was never so relieved to see anyone in my life. I realized that night I was in love with you."

"Kalinda, my love…" he breathed as if a great weight had been lifted from his shoulders. She felt the relief in him.

"Do you really love me?" She pulled back, lifting her hands to frame his face. He smiled at her, a heart-stopping look of love that told her everything.

"You do, don't you?" she said wonderingly.

"With all my heart." It was a solemn vow. "Didn't you realize that when I rigged the engagement? I did it more for my own sake than to ward off Hutton's bribery tactics. I figured once I'd gotten you past the shock of the idea I could talk you into it on reasonable grounds. Instead, I wound up seducing you into it," he ended with a groan of self-recrimination. "I should never have done that. It wasn't right. But I wanted you so much.…"

"The sneaky seduction tactics were so successful because I wanted nothing more in the world than to marry you!" she assured him, eyes filled with fond laughter.

"I wonder if you have any idea how important

you are to me? You told me you were afraid I'd only followed you back to Denver because you'd made me realize I wanted to come back to this world. And I couldn't argue with your conclusion because it was true in a very real sense. But you didn't understand the whole truth, Kalinda. I wouldn't have wanted to come back without you. I would have found the business life just as empty, just as destructive for me as it had been before.''

"Oh, Rand..."

"It's true, sweetheart. I do have the business instincts of a shark. I learned a lot about myself up there in the mountains, faced some important facts. I need that easy, contemplative side of life and I need the high-powered entrepreneurial side. But it wasn't until I met you that I realized I had a chance of having both.''

"I don't understand." She looked up at him wistfully.

"Don't you see? You're more important to me than either of those two lifestyles. You're the most important thing in my life. And that puts things into perspective, making it possible to have it all. If I can have you.''

"Every time I look at that beautiful piece of pottery you made I realize I love the man who made it just as much as the man who saved Brady Data Processing. And you're not the only greedy one,

Rand," Kalinda smiled. "I want it all, too. I want you. I love you."

His hands moved yearningly along her back as he stared down at her. He looked as if he didn't fully trust his luck, Kalinda decided. But she was the lucky one. How could she have ever run away that morning in the mountains?

"I'll take care of you, Kalinda," he promised. "I love you so much. I *need* you so much. I need you to keep me from drinking too much coffee, to keep me from falling into the trap of becoming a business shark, to keep me from an empty, incomplete life."

"And I need you. A man I can trust, a man I can rely on for sound, rational advice, a man who wants me more than trout fishing or empire building." Her lips quirked invitingly, gently. "Love me, Rand. Please love me."

He folded her to him, a reverence and a deep desire forming opposite ends of the spectrum which constituted his love for her. Kalinda felt it and reveled in it, giving herself up eagerly to the urgent need to share the love they had.

"I think," he rasped close to her ear as he tugged at the comb that held her hair, "the president of Brady Data Processing should take a little time off now that the immediate crisis is past, don't you?"

She shivered as her hair tumbled down her shoulders, aware of his hands moving through the golden-brown stuff with masculine delight. "A vacation?"

"I was thinking more in terms of a honeymoon," he replied, slipping off the jacket of her suit. "It so happens I know of a delightful mountain retreat situated picturesquely on the bank of a scenic lake...."

"Indoor facilities, I trust?"

"Only the finest," he assured her simply, removing her small-collared blouse as she began fumbling with the buttons of his shirt. "Fresh trout in the morning, arts and crafts in the afternoon, daily picnics."

"It sounds charming."

As her lacy bra slid to the carpet, Rand groaned and crushed her to his naked chest. "It is charming. But to tell you the truth, the place has always lacked something."

"A woman's touch?" She nibbled suggestively at the curve of his throat.

"Not just any woman's touch," he murmured. "Your touch. Will you come back to the mountains for a honeymoon with me, Kalinda?" he begged, as they stepped out of the last of their clothes. "I promise you won't be bored."

"I wasn't bored last time, not after I met you," she confessed as he molded her body to his own. She trailed her nails sensuously down his back, feeling the instant response of his body. "But don't you think that tempting the president of the company with visions of a weekend in the mountains may constitute some sort of corporate bribery?''

"Haven't you learned anything at all about me?'' he whispered thickly, lifting her and carrying her over to the sun-dappled couch. "Ask anyone in town, they'll all tell you I'm a man who will stop at nothing to get what I want!''

"As long as I'm what you want." She smiled up at him through her lashes, pulling his mouth down to hers.

"You're the only thing I really want. The only thing that counts."

And then he was demonstrating the wonder and depths of his love to the woman who had developed a passionate love for a shark.

SPECIAL EDITION

Stories of love and life, these powerful novels are tales that you can identify with—romances with "something special" added in!

Fall in love with the stories of authors such as **Nora Roberts, Diana Palmer, Ginna Gray** and many more of your special favorites—as well as wonderful new voices!

Special Edition brings you entertainment for the heart!

SILHOUETTE®

Desire®

Do you want...

Dangerously handsome heroes

Evocative, everlasting love stories

Sizzling and tantalizing sensuality

Incredibly sexy miniseries like **MAN OF THE MONTH**

Red-hot romance

Enticing entertainment that can't be beat!

You'll find all of this, and much *more* each and every month in **SILHOUETTE DESIRE**. Don't miss these unforgettable love stories by some of romance's hottest authors. Silhouette Desire—where your fantasies will always come true....

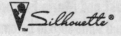

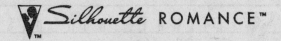

What's a single dad to do when he needs a wife by next Thursday?

Who's a confirmed bachelor to call when he finds a baby on his doorstep?

How does a plain Jane in love with her gorgeous boss get him to notice her?

From classic love stories to romantic comedies to emotional heart tuggers, **Silhouette Romance** offers six irresistible novels every month by some of your favorite authors! Such as...beloved bestsellers **Diana Palmer, Annette Broadrick, Suzanne Carey, Elizabeth August** and **Marie Ferrarella,** to name just a few—and some sure to become favorites!

Fabulous Fathers...Bundles of Joy...Miniseries... Months of blushing brides and convenient weddings... Holiday celebrations... You'll find all this and much more in **Silhouette Romance**—always emotional, always enjoyable, always about love!

SR-GEN

WAYS TO UNEXPECTEDLY MEET MR. RIGHT:

♡ *Go out with the sexy-sounding stranger your daughter secretly set you up with through a personal ad.*

♡ *RSVP yes to a wedding invitation—soon it might be your turn to say "I do!"*

♡ *Receive a marriage proposal by mail— from a man you've never met....*

These are just a few of the unexpected ways that written communication leads to love in Silhouette Yours Truly.

Each month, look for two fast-paced, fun and flirtatious Yours Truly novels (with entertaining treats and sneak previews in the back pages) by some of your favorite authors—and some who are sure to become favorites.

YOURS TRULY™:
Love—when you least expect it!

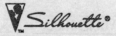

YT-GEN